THE LONE GREYHOUND

Dick rode out into the desert. He halted on the slope of a hill that overlooked a water hole, tied Croppy to a palo verde, and with the .22 in his hands made his way to the rim of the hill. He didn't expect to see anything, for few desert dwellers moved about when the sun was hot. But there was always a chance of surprising something. He came to the top and stood quietly behind a big saguaro.

Presently he saw a coyote and kept intent eyes on it. There was a ten-dollar bounty on coyotes, but this one was hopelessly out of the .22's effective range. However, it might come nearer and he wanted to be ready.

What at first he thought was a wolf, but presently recognized as a greyhound, flashed into sight and hurled itself at the coyote. Dick stood spellbound, his eyes fixed on the fleet, tawny dog. Then it faded from sight in the greasewood.

What was a lone greyhound doing in the desert?

Desert Dog
by Jim Kjelgaard

A BANTAM SKYLARK® BOOK
Toronto · New York · London · Sydney

DESERT DOG

*A Bantam Skylark Book / published by arrangement with
Holiday House*

PRINTING HISTORY

*Holiday House edition published August 1956
9 printings through September 1971*

Bantam Skylark edition / September 1979

ISBN 0-553-15013-8

Published simultaneously in the United States and Canada

*Bantam Books are published by Bantam Books, Inc. Its trade-
mark, consisting of the word "Bantam Books" and the por-
trayal of a bantam, is Registered in U.S. Patent and Trademark
Office and in other countries, Marca Registrada. Bantam
Books, Inc., 666 Fifth Avenue, New York, New York 10019.*

PRINTED IN THE UNITED STATES OF AMERICA

0 9 8 7 6 5 4 3 2

To Christine

Contents

Desert Dog

1. Fred Haver

Tawny shivered, not understanding this and not liking it because he did not understand. When the wheeling buzzard dipped closer, Tawny snarled fiercely and the short hair on his neck bristled. The buzzard soared higher and Tawny returned to where Fred Haver lay among the crushed branches of greasewood.

Whining low in his throat, Tawny thrust a slim muzzle against his friend. Getting no response, he pawed very gently but anxiously at the man's rumpled jacket. He raised his head suddenly, fearing that the buzzard might have descended again. But it was still soaring patiently, maintaining its altitude.

His eyes fixed on the buzzard, Tawny stood motionless. His short ears were erect, his greyhound body, still showing traces of puppyhood, was tense and rigid. His grey-brown, smoke-colored short hair blended into the desert background. A hundred feet beyond him, a giant saguaro cactus thrust its many-armed trunk toward the sky. Beyond that was more desert that rose to cactus-studded, near-treeless hills. For a moment Tawny let his eyes rest on the hills, while within him rose the strange stirring that he always felt when he looked into uncluttered space. Scarcely seeming to move his head, he looked again at the buzzard.

Tawny came of what is probably the oldest breed of dog known to man, and ages had changed him little. Heavy of chest and lean of paunch, with a spear-shaped head and a slim tail, he had wonderfully long legs which, though slender, were strong and hard. His remote ancestors had been tamed because, lacking any weapons except stones and spears, ancient man needed a dog intelligent enough to work closely with him, fast enough to run down the speediest game, and courageous enough to fight and hold his game after he caught it.

The young greyhound bent his head to look squarely into Fred Haver's face, and the worry in his eyes became more intense. Tawny had a mighty love for three things: speed, freedom, and the man who now lay motionless in the greasewood.

Earlier this morning Fred Haver had taken him from his kennel, whistled him into the pickup truck that was used to carry the kennel dogs, and brought him out into the desert. This trip for an exercise period in the desert was routine. But they had gone scarcely a hundred yards from the truck when Fred had cried out, stumbled, and fallen. Nor had he moved since. It was beyond the dog's understanding. He looked around anxiously.

Three hundred yards away, a mule deer that had already browsed its fill and been to water, rested in the shelter of a dry wash. Long-eared jack rabbits went about their various affairs. Gophers ventured a few yards from their dens, then squeaked and scurried back. A heavy-bodied rattlesnake, just emerged from its winter's den, coiled near a clump of cholla cactus and waited for a pack rat to venture from its spiny nest.

All these things would have been evident to a hound, setter, cur, or any dog with a keen nose, for such dogs would have read the wind currents. Tawny knew about none of them for it was not his nature to use his nose. He was one of the so-called 'gaze hounds' who run by sight alone.

But his sight was remarkable and presently it was called into play.

All about him was a sea of greasewood broken here and there by cactus: stately saguaro, ocotillo with its serpentine withes, prickly pear, spiny cholla, and hook-studded barrel. But there were avenues and passages where it was possible to see through the greasewood. Down one of these passages was the coyote, as far as two city blocks away when Tawny saw it.

The coyote was slinking, crouching low to the ground and moving slowly because by so doing it hoped to remain unseen. The coyote had smelled Fred Haver and Tawny, knew something had gone amiss, and with the usual bent of its kind, was coming to see if it could turn another's misfortune to its own advantage.

Tawny followed with his eyes, losing the coyote at times and at other times seeing it only as a flitting patch of grey fur that appeared here and there. But he knew it was coming nearer. When the coyote was ninety yards away, Tawny launched his attack.

He sprang suddenly, taking so little time to get under way that he developed full speed with almost his first couple of bounds. He kept his head high the better to see, and his eyes never wavered from the coyote. Uncertain at once as to just what happened, the coyote lingered a moment. Then it turned to flee. An old animal that knew most of a coyote's many tricks, this one knew that there was no time for strategy now. It would have to depend on its legs because the dog was coming very fast, but the coyote knew and had confidence in its own speed. It could run away from most things.

But in spite of its fifty-yard start—Tawny had run forty yards while the coyote was making up its mind—it could not run away from Tawny. Four hundred yards from where it had started to run, with Tawny a bare half-dozen leaps behind, the coyote whipped about with its back against a rock and made ready to fight for its life.

Its fur was bristled to make it look bigger and fiercer. Its ears were flattened. Its face was a snarling mask. Its jaws snapped continuously with a sound like that of a springing steel trap. Its tail was curved between its legs and lying flat against the belly. Most men would have interpreted that as a sign of cravenness, but Tawny knew better instinctively. The coyote held its tail in such a position because, should there be a belly attack in the forthcoming fight, the enemy would bite its tail first, instead of the vulnerable belly.

With no slackening of speed, Tawny leaped in. But though he seemed intent on meeting the coyote squarely, at the last second, so fast and with such a superb muscular control that there was not the slightest fumble, he launched a flank attack instead. His slicing teeth cut through grey fur and into the flesh beneath while the coyote's own slash missed entirely.

Its nerve breaking, the coyote whirled and fled. About to pursue farther, Tawny checked himself. His blood was up and he did not fear to fight. But he had run a long way from his helpless friend. Letting the coyote go, Tawny raced full speed back to Fred Haver.

Back at the man's side, Tawny glanced up at the still-wheeling buzzard, then softly nosed his friend's motionless body and licked his face with a soft, warm tongue.

The dog felt forlorn, hopeless, lost. Tawny knew how to cope with a coyote, or any enemy into which he could set his teeth. But he was helpless in the face of this strange situation, and he expressed his desperate unhappiness with a miserable little whine. Crouching full length, he pillowed his slim head on Fred Haver's shoulder.

He dared not lie quietly for very long because of his uncertainty and the unknown perils that beset him. Fred Haver was helpless and unable to protect himself. Therefore, Tawny must protect him. So he searched the desert constantly, marking in his own mind a line beyond which nothing would be allowed to venture. He kept an especially wary eye on the buzzard. Its intentions were all too plain and so was its patience. Buzzards are seldom in a hurry, for what they want will always wait.

Tawny looked again at the far peaks and was stirred by their challenge. But even though he yearned toward them because they represented unlimited space, the ties that bound him to Fred Haver were too powerful to break. He must stay here because this was his place.

When a hopping jack rabbit appeared, he eyed it suspiciously. But the big rabbit veered off before it passed the line Tawny had marked, and he paid no more attention to it.

It was late afternoon before there was another interruption.

Tawny heard the car grinding in second gear over the same desert path that Fred Haver had taken with the pickup truck. Leaping up, the better to see over the greasewood, Tawny saw the approaching vehicle. It was a sleek and shiny black car, but in the blue shadows cast by the oblique rays of the setting sun, it assumed a purplish hue. The car stopped beside the truck and two men Tawny knew got out.

One was Charles Northcott, who often visited the kennels where Tawny was kept with other greyhounds and who seemed to have much authority there. Tawny did not know that Charles Northcott owned the kennels of racing greyhounds, and he wouldn't have cared if he had known. The dog could give his allegiance to only one man and he had given it to Fred Haver.

The second man was John Weston, who trained and raced greyhounds of his own.

Tawny watched them hopefully, joyously, and for the first time since Fred Haver had fallen, his spirits rose. In Tawny's brief experience, humans were all wise and all powerful. These two men would do what he failed to do; make Fred Haver get up and walk again.

Unobtrusively, partly because it was his nature and partly because he had never felt the slightest attachment for anyone or anything except his fallen friend, Tawny waited for them. But his eyes were anxious and beseeching, as he looked up at the two men.

Tawny moved aside while they knelt to examine Fred Haver. They rose, and Tawny knew a terrible moment when the fallen man did not rise with them.

"The poor cuss!" Charles Northcott said.

There was genuine sorrow in his voice. He was the wealthy owner and Fred Haver only his trainer, but between them there had been a bond that rose above money and social position. Above all else, Fred Haver loved a fine greyhound and had taught Charles Northcott how to appreciate one, too.

"Heart, do you think?" John Weston asked somberly.

Northcott nodded. "He's had heart trouble for some time. The doctor warned him a year ago to take it easy."

John Weston looked down at the still body. "I can't imagine him taking it easy as long as there were greyhounds to be trained."

"That's right. They were his whole life."

Tawny whined, trying in his own way to return their attention to the plight of his friend. They looked at him, and as men will when they are faced with big things about which they can do nothing, they spoke of little ones.

"Nice looking pup," John Weston commented.

"Fred said he had the makings of a great racer."

"What's his name?"

"Tawny Streak."

John Weston looked at Tawny again. He too had an insight into greyhounds, and had trained many good ones.

"Looks to me as though he may be a bit spooky. Maybe some bronco in that pup?"

"I haven't paid much attention to the pups," Charles Northcott admitted. "Fred seemed to get along with him."

"Fred got along with all greyhounds," John Weston declared. "The racing circuit won't be the same without him."

They stood silently for a short space, as though they did not want to concede failure and were casting about for something they could do. Charles Northcott finally broke the awkward silence that had come between them.

"We might as well get going."

"Might as well."

They brought a robe from the car and wrapped all that was left of Fred Haver in it. Self-consciously, as though unsure as to whether or not they were doing the right thing, they laid the blanketed form in the pickup truck.

"Will you drive him in?" Northcott asked.

"Sure."

Tawny danced anxiously, looking up at the place

where his friend rested and yearning to be beside him once more. But, so sobered by the death of his trainer that he was almost unaware of what he was doing, Charles Northcott snapped a leash on the dog's collar. Trained to obey a leash, Tawny stood still.

He watched closely while John Weston turned the truck around and drove back toward the highway. When Northcott opened the rear door of his big car and snapped his fingers, Tawny climbed in. He did so automatically, having been taught to obey the wishes of humans.

He climbed on the cushioned rear seat, his eyes still fixed upon the truck that carried Fred Haver. They came to a concrete highway and the truck faded into a stream of traffic. Nervous and worried, Tawny looked intently at each passing car. But not again did he see the truck.

His spirits rose when Charles Northcott stopped beside the big building that housed the rest of his greyhounds, for Tawny hoped that Fred Haver would meet him there. Instead, the car was met by an old, gaunt roustabout known to his employer as Billy and to his intimates on the greyhound circuit as Billy the Kid. Northcott got out and gave him Tawny's leash.

"Put him away, will you, Billy?"

"Shore." Billy squinted with his one good eye. "Whar's Fred?"

"He won't be coming back," Charles Northcott said soberly. "He had a heart attack out on the desert."

"Now hain't that a sad thing."

There was a veiled elation in Billy's voice, for he himself cherished a secret desire to be Charles Northcott's trainer. He never could be, because really outstanding greyhound men were born, not made. Billy led Tawny into the gloomy, unlighted building.

"Come 'long. Come 'long, purp."

Tawny followed only because the leash was still on his collar and he had been taught to obey. But as far as he was concerned, Billy was only another kennel boy who brought him his carefully prepared and rationed meals, provided him with fresh water, and under Fred Haver's watchful eye, rubbed him down.

Voluntarily Tawny entered his kennel, more properly a cage closed by a steel-barred door. Tired out, he lay down in the bed of freshly torn newspapers that awaited him. When a greyhound runs he gives all and Tawny had had a hard, fast run after the coyote. Ordinarily he would have gone to sleep at once, but he was still too worried to sleep.

He was aware of his various kennel mates that ranged from six as yet unproven pups like himself to the redoubtable King Bee, the pride of Charles Northcott's kennel. With one full year of racing behind him, King had run a standard five-sixteenths of a mile, or five hundred and fifty yards, in just a shade over thirty-one seconds, and had won purses totaling more than twenty thousand dollars. In all likelihood, King's second year would be better. His owner had been offered, and refused, seven thousand five hundred dollars for him.

Tawny paid little attention to any of the other dogs for he had little regard for any of them. It was not in him to give lavishly of himself. The dogs in the kennel with him meant no more than Billy the Kid, John Weston, Charles Northcott, or the puppies his own age against which he had raced. Except for Fred Haver, everything was part of a pattern. But the pattern merely existed; it had no real meaning.

He brightened eagerly when he heard the kennel door open and someone enter. Then he relaxed sadly. Billy, and not Fred Haver, had come into the kennel.

Without great interest or much appetite, Tawny ate the meal Billy put in the kennel, and lay down again.

Finally he slept. His paws twitched eagerly in his sleep, for a dream had come to him. He was out on the desert with Fred Haver, but instead of coming back to the kennel after his prescribed exercise period was over, they stayed on the desert. Trucks, cars, kennels, uniformed handlers, spectators, music, all the artificial aspects of greyhound racing were left far and forever behind. There was only space in which to exercise his legs, and together he and Fred Haver went into the mountains that loomed so enticingly on the horizon.

But when he awakened, he was still in the dark kennel. Tawny heard another greyhound get up, turn restlessly, and seek a more comfortable position. At the far end of the kennel, a lonesome puppy whined. When Tawny went back to sleep, he was more contented. Morning was on its way, and morning always brought Fred Haver.

Tawny went into another happy dream. He was racing, striving his utmost to catch the mechanical rabbit that bobbed on a steel track before him. He knew instinctively that the rabbit was not real but he knew also that other dogs were striving to catch it, too, and he must be first. These two things, a born love of speed and the spirit of competition, summed up Tawny's knowledge of racing.

He did not know that a greyhound starts to race when it is about fifteen or sixteen months old, and that thereafter its racing life is about two years. He did not understand that, on northern tracks in summer and on southern or southwestern courses in winter, a greyhound in prime condition can run about twice a week. Nor could he have the faintest idea of a greyhound's fate when its racing usefulness is over.

A few beloved dogs are kept as pets, a few are given away, and a few are kept for breeding, with no guarantee whatsoever that a sire or dam with a notable track record will beget sons and daughters equally as fast. The rest of the greyhounds that have outlived their racing usefulness are painlessly put to sleep. This is not merely a convenient method for getting rid of unwanted dogs. Racing greyhounds are among the most pampered of animals and most owners love their dogs greatly. It troubles an owner to think of his cherished racers, that have had every possible attention, in the hands of new owners who may give them little or no care.

Tawny did not understand that there is almost no possibility of using underhanded methods in order to insure that some favorite dog will win a race. Racing greyhounds carry no jockeys. They run for the love of running and the best dog wins. Greyhound tracks are under the supervision of experienced officials who know what they're about, and anyone caught trying to prearrange the results of any race is barred forever from all tracks.

Tawny knew only that he dreamed of freedom, adored speed, and loved Fred Haver. He needed all three elements to make him completely happy, and at present he had none.

When morning came again, it was Billy who brought his water and cleaned out his cage. Tawny waited sadly, ears alert for every sound and eyes close to the grilled bars of his kennel door. Every morning each dog in the kennel went out for exercise, and Tawny was among the favored ones that went with Fred Haver. But this morning nobody took any of the dogs out, and Tawny turned restlessly around and around in his kennel. When he ran, he ran terrifically, and such exertion took its toll. But being young, he recuperated swiftly and soon felt the need to run again. Abundant energy needed an outlet, and today there was none.

That made him restless and nervous, so that he had no taste for his evening meal when it was offered to him. He needed room in the same sense that a hawk needs it, and the kennel was barely big enough to permit his turning around. Billy took away his untasted food and Tawny inspected every inch of his kennel. When a piece of paper wafted into the air before him, he snatched it in his jaws and shook it fiercely, as he might have shaken some live thing he had caught.

That night, having been deprived of their usual run and missing it greatly, all the dogs were restless. Some moaned their disquiet to the uncaring darkness, but Tawny remained still. Just as he had given his entire affection to Fred Haver, so he had placed his whole trust in him. Now that Fred was no longer here, he trusted only himself.

The next morning he had only a passing glance for Billy when he cleaned his kennel and shut the door. Standing motionless against the grill, Tawny centered his whole attention on the door leading into the shed. Mutely, hopelessly, but with every taut nerve in his body, he yearned for Fred Haver.

When the door finally opened, it was Charles Northcott and John Weston who came in.

Tawny watched them steadily, unnoticed himself because he was one of many dogs and because he held so still. He sensed something about Charles Northcott that had not been there before, a sad and dreary something. Though Northcott had never understood his dogs as Fred Haver did, he had at least been partly in tune with them. Now, when he entered the kennel, he did so as an alien and every dog sensed it.

"That's the story," he was saying. "Fred and I made a pretty decent team, but now that he's gone the fun's gone too. So I'm selling."

"I understand," John Weston said quietly, "and I appreciate your giving me first chance. I'll take King Bee, as I said."

"He'll be worth it three times over this coming season."

"If," John Weston smiled, "he doesn't lame a paw, or sicken, or run his heart out."

"I know," the other admitted. "A man's crazy to take a chance on a greyhound."

John Weston shrugged. "Some of us are born crazy. I'll take King Bee and glad to get him, and I'll send you my check. Otherwise I have a pretty full kennel, though if I didn't I'd be tempted by that Tawny pup Fred had out when we found him."

"You like Tawny, eh?"

"Not particularly. To me he's just another youngster. But if Fred Haver said he's got something, he's got it."

"Let's have another look at him," Charles Northcott said. "Get Tawny out, will you, Billy?"

Wholly indifferent to all three men, but obedient to the leash that Billy snapped on his collar, Tawny left his kennel and stood quietly for John Weston's inspection. After a moment, Weston turned to Northcott.

"He's going to be one of two things: a champion or an out and out renegade. There isn't going to be any in-between for him."

"What do you mean, John?"

"The dog may have it," Weston conceded, "and if Fred Haver had lived he might have made a second King Bee out of the pup. But I'm sure the bronco streak's still there. He doesn't give a hang about any of us or much of anything else. I might be able to win him over, and then again I might not. Right now he belongs to himself and may never change. If he doesn't he'll be more of a liability than an asset to anyone who owns him. But he interests me. I'd like to see him run."

"He's entered in the puppy elimination Wednesday night. Why don't you watch him race before you make up your mind?"

"Fair enough. I'll meet you at the track," John Weston promised.

2. Puppy Stake

John Weston was a patient man. Because of that, because he was willing to work until he understood a problem, because he was able patiently to sift through a mass of tedious detail to find the hard, usable core of what he wanted, he had a reputation around the greyhound tracks for second sight. Frequently, it was said, he knew what a dog was going to do before the dog did.

The reputation was absurd, and nobody knew that better than John Weston. Understanding of anything started with love for it, and he loved a fine greyhound. But behind him was also twenty years of study, during which he had not only watched thousands of greyhounds run but had carefully analyzed the reasons for their success or failure. Unlike many owners, he never trusted his dogs entirely to any trainer or hired handler, but supervised them himself. Nobody could teach a greyhound how to run for that came naturally, but much of John Weston's success resulted because he himself attended the thousand and one details connected with that running. He maintained a comparatively small kennel, and every day personally inspected each dog. He knew what they were eating, where the food came from, how it was mixed, whether or not any dog might be a bit out of condition, and each one's individual quirks and foibles.

Tonight, as he walked with the crowd that was rapidly filling the grandstand of the Wilmo Greyhound Track, he wished that he did have some magical insight. If he did, he would know whether or not to add Tawny to his kennel.

Tawny was fast because Fred Haver had said so: Fred had seldom been wrong about greyhounds. But speed alone did not make a champion, and John Weston had an instinctive distrust of something about Tawny. It was nothing he could see, but he sensed it strongly. Was it that Tawny would give everything he had only if the right master were with him to call it forth? Or was it that Tawny had a real bronco streak? John Weston could not afford to have such a dog in his kennel. He'd spent too many years building up his reputation to risk ruining it with a renegade.

Entering the grandstand, he bought a program and scanned it. The first six of tonight's ten races were merely conventional five-hundred-and-fifty-yard turns around the track, with the dogs in each race grouped according to the speed they had shown in previous races. The seventh was one of the elimination races for the Wilmo Puppy Stake, in which eighty-one dogs that had not yet reached their second birthday would run. But seventy-two would be eliminated in these trial heats, and the nine dogs that eventually ran the Puppy Stake would naturally be the pick of the lot.

"Evening, John."

Smiling, Charles Northcott detached himself from the crowd and came forward. John Weston smiled back.

"Hi, Charley. Let's go look at the dogs."

They made their way to the glass-enclosed kennel room where the ninety dogs that would run in tonight's ten races were being kept until it was time for them to go out. All dogs must be delivered to the kennel room three hours before track time, and were thereafter completely out of their owners' hands until the race on which they were to run was over.

The ten dogs that would run in the first race had been taken out of their kennel boxes, muzzled, and each covered with a light blanket bearing the number of his track position. Reacting according to their natures, some sat almost listlessly, some were tense and alert, one padded restlessly as far as a short leash would let him go, and one gave voice to a succession of excited yelps. Peering at the wooden kennel boxes, John Weston finally saw Tawny.

The pup was at the far side of the room, in the upper tier of kennels. He was lying down, but his head was up and his ears alert as he followed with quick eyes every motion in the kennel room.

Weston pointed. "There he is."

"Where?"

"Top row, third kennel from the far end."

"Oh, yes, I see him. He's an independent-looking cuss, isn't he?"

"A lot of dogs are, but in not quite the same way. Charley, I just can't figure that hound!"

Northcott grinned. "Still looking for the bronco streak?"

"Not just looking for it. I'm seeing it!"

"How do you know?"

"I don't, really. Call it a hunch."

"And do you believe in hunches?"

"How can I help it? I've been a greyhound man for twenty years."

Led by their uniformed captain, the handlers in charge of dogs in the first race started toward the track.

"The dogs are coming out for the first race," the loud-speaker blared.

"Let's watch," Weston suggested. "There are some good dogs in this race."

Single file, the handlers paraded their dogs toward the starting boxes, reversed to go in the other direction, walked almost around the track, and put the dogs in their boxes. As the handlers left the track, the loud-speaker announced, "Here comes the rabbit."

No rabbit at all, but a mechanical contrivance that moved on an electrically operated axle, the rabbit bounced past and the starting boxes were opened si-multaneously. The dogs rushed out and began their futile attempt to catch the rabbit which, no matter how fast they ran, would always move a little faster. Finally the rabbit scuttled back into its den and the number 4 flashed in the winner's space on the electric bulletin board across the track.

"Good race," John Weston said. "Number Four is Duke Harry. I'd like to see him in a race with King Bee."

There were no outstanding dogs in the next race, so John Weston and Charles Northcott sipped coffee in the snack bar. There they talked of past races they had seen and great dogs they had known. Finally the loud-speaker drew their attention.

"The seventh race, a puppy elimination race, is now coming up."

John Weston glanced briefly at his program to see the post positions of the nine pups. The rail on which the rabbit skipped was on the inside of the track's oval, and post position was important. Number One was on the inside, closest to the rabbit, and the dog in that position had a little better chance than any of the rest. The second and third positions were the next best, for the dogs starting from those had to cross in front of only one or two of their track mates in order to gain the favored inside of the track. The dogs starting from positions four to eight were at a handicap because they must of necessity mingle with the pack. Number Nine was another good post. Though he had eight dogs on the inside, the starter from nine had nothing on the other side, and that allowed him comparative freedom of movement.

Number One was Black Bart, a good dog, but not exceptional. Two was Sarawak Queen, and a dog named Conquistador would start from the third position. Conquistador was a big dog, weighing seventy-seven pounds, but he looked fast. Tawny was Number Six.

Weston looked at the lighted sign upon which were listed the post positions, the present odds of each dog, track time, and other pertinent data. Obviously the favorite, Black Bart was two to one. Next in line, Conquistador was three to one, and a brindle dog named Sally's Pride, starting from Number Nine, was third. Tawny was listed at nine to one.

John Weston's eyes sought out Tawny. The pup still seemed apart, belonging very much to himself, walking beside his handler only because of the leash. But there was about him a vibrant eagerness and an air of anticipation, that had nothing to do with the lights, the color, or the pageantry.

All these, John Weston understood, were for the benefit of human spectators. Tawny trembled with excitement because he was going to run again and knew it. John Weston sighed, seeing in Tawny a part of what Fred Haver had said was there. If such a dog, with so much to give, would give it for love of a new master as well as for love of speed, he might be unbeatable.

Charles Northcott turned to Weston. "He looks good, doesn't he?"

"They all look good."

Keeping an almost military step, the handlers paraded their dogs past the grandstand and turned stiffly to start back around the track. There was a momentary pause as, in turn, each dog's muzzle was inspected by the track captain. During the pause the loud-speaker announced the dogs' numbers, names, weights, and owners. Still in step, moving slowly, the procession went almost the length of the track.

John Weston's eyes remained on Tawny, but in a detached manner he noticed the others. Sally's Pride decided that Conquistador was just the playmate he had been looking for, and did his best to start a frolic with him. A dog named Fancy Jean, thinking she saw motion on the other side of the track, leaped to the end of her leash and fought when the handler brought her up short. But Tawny walked stiffly, as though he were the only living creature on the track. Weston knew that the pup was not posing. As far as Tawny was concerned, there were no other dogs or men. He was, as usual, holding himself aloof. He cared only about the forth-coming race.

The handlers led their dogs to the starting box, which actually did resemble a long box with numbers on the front. But it was separated into nine compartments and so arranged that the nine gates in front all opened at exactly the same instant. All dogs had an equal chance to start. From the rear the handlers thrust their dogs into the compartments that corresponded with the numbers they had drawn. Then, for the first time, the handlers broke their parade-ground formation. They ran toward the grandstand and scrambled off the track.

"Here comes the rabbit," announced the loudspeaker.

Riding its steel path, the rabbit began to bounce around the track. The grandstand was dimmed and only the track remained lighted. When the rabbit was about fifteen yards ahead of the starting box, the dogs were released.

John Weston held his breath. The start of any greyhound race was a crucial time. Some dogs were ready to
go at once and some needed a split second to get under
way. It made a great difference for, in greyhound racing, there is seldom more than a split second between
the winners and losers.

Pressed closely by Conquistador, Sarawak Queen
took the early lead and increased it. The grandstand
became filled with excited murmuring as spectators
vocally urged their favorite to win. A laugh went up as
Black Bart, off to a slow start, stopped to sniff inter-
estedly at something on the track. Finally realizing that
he was in a race, but hopelessly outdistanced, he ran to
catch up with the rest.

Tangled in the pack, Tawny was running sixth.

Unbeatable for a short sprint but without stamina for
a long race, Sarawak Queen fell behind. Some booed
her, but John Weston felt a pang of pity. He knew how
much Sarawak Queen had given in the first hundred
and fifty yards and understood why she fell behind.
Conquistador surged ahead until his lean grey length
flashed a full eighteen inches in front of the rest. Sally's
Pride, starting from Number Nine position, strained
neck and neck with Fancy Jean for second place.

Suddenly Tawny was running with something besides his legs. His brain and heart were in it too. He was
again a hunter's dog and must catch his game. It made
no difference if it was only a mechanical rabbit; it was
still a challenge. Unable to maintain the terrific pace,
Fancy Jean fell behind. Inch by inch, Tawny closed the
distance between himself and Sally's Pride.

Then the race was over.

The grandstand lights came on. Across the track, John
Weston watched the winners' numbers flash onto the
bulletin board. First was 3, Conquistador, the winner.
Next was 9 for Sally's Pride, then 6 for Tawny. John

Weston stood spellbound, knowing that he had witnessed a great performance. Tawny hadn't won, but when he had suddenly put his heart in the race, he had surged magnificently ahead, showing great staying power.

"What do you think of him now?" Charles Northcott said happily.

"I always thought well of him. If he'd do that every time, he'd be another King Bee in a few months."

"Still worried?"

"I still see the bronco in him," Weston confessed. "There's something strange about that dog. Maybe he'll outgrow it. Perhaps he's grieving for Fred. Or maybe he really is wild. I'd like to see what he does on the desert, off the track. Can we take him there?"

"Sure. How about tomorrow?"

"Tomorrow will be fine," John Weston said. "Suppose I pick you up at half-past eight?"

Awakening only now and again to find a more comfortable position, or to lap a little fresh water and eat his dinner, Tawny slept for eight hours. But when he finally awoke, he was wholly rested. He rose and peered between the bars on his kennel door.

He would like to run again, for only in running had he found satisfaction. The possibility of another race and only that, now kept him interested. Fred Haver had not visited him in a very long while and Tawny ached for him. He also longed for the sense of freedom and space that his trips to the desert with Fred had brought.

Tawny glanced indifferently at the lackadaisical Billy, who was cleaning a kennel at the far end of the line. King Bee had already gone to John Weston's kennel and some of the other dogs had also been sold. Tawny did not miss them. He regarded them much the same as he did Billy, just a part of things, part of the pattern of life as Tawny knew it. But except for racing, it had become a drab pattern.

There was a little more interest in his eyes when Charles Northcott and John Weston came into the building. Tawny was not really drawn to either man, but both had always treated him kindly. Much more important, they were the last two humans Tawny knew who had had anything to do with Fred Haver.

Charles Northcott opened the door to Tawny's kennel and snapped his fingers softly. "Come on out, Tawny."

Tawny stepped out, took the tidbit, a tiny piece of fresh hamburger, that Northcott offered him, and acknowledged the gift with a slight wag of his tail. Then he stared straight ahead as Northcott snapped a leash on his collar and started toward the door.

When ordered, Tawny climbed into the back seat of John Weston's car and sat quietly until he realized that they were not going to the track but out in the desert. Then he began to tremble with excitement. Fred Haver had always exercised him in the desert, and this was the first time he'd been there since Fred's death.

He made no move to get out of the car when it finally stopped because Fred Haver had taught him manners. But when Northcott opened the car door, Tawny leaped out eagerly. Unsnapping the leash, Northcott waved his hand.

"All right, Tawny. Go ahead."

Tawny walked a few steps, then broke into a fast run that carried him a hundred yards. When the wind carried a piece of torn paper in front of him, he leaped to snap it up. Then he stopped to look around. He had no recollection of having been in this exact spot at any previous time, yet the place seemed familiar.

Ready to run again, he responded instantly to the

piercing whistle when Charles Northcott blew it. Though he had never loved anyone except Fred Haver, the bonds that tied him to men were strong and unquestionable. He must respond to the whistle because he had been so trained, but at the same time he was very restless. He turned to the two men reluctantly.

"Is he still the bronco?" Northcott asked.

John Weston looked puzzled. "He certainly doesn't act it now."

Tawny saw the jack rabbit before either man was aware of it, hopping out of some greasewood fifty yards away. Tawny strained eagerly, head up and eyes questing. Following his gaze, John Weston saw the big desert hare.

"Reckon he can catch it?"

"Let's find out. Take him, Tawny!"

The dog flashed forward, and had covered a third of the distance when the jack rabbit saw him coming. It dashed away, skittering up a small knoll on the summit of which grew a lonely ironwood tree. Eyes on the rabbit, Tawny mounted the knoll. The rabbit dodged sidewise but Tawny ran straight ahead.

This time he paid no attention whatever to the summoning whistle, for from the top of the knoll he saw, a quarter of a mile away, the many-armed saguaro near where Fred Haver had always parked the truck. Rising beyond that was the rocky knoll where Fred usually rested while Tawny ran. This was well-remembered country, a dear place, and Tawny whined low in his throat as he streaked toward it. He heard the whistle's summoning blast again, but again paid no attention whatever to it.

He reached and raced up the rocky knoll. There he leaped high, throat tense and tail stiff as he looked. His eyes were wild with excitement. This was where he had last seen Fred Haver and, since there was no trace of him elsewhere, it followed that this was where he would find him. Quivering with eagerness, Tawny coursed around the rocky knoll like a trail hound on a scent. A dozen times he went to where Fred had fallen in the greasewood.

When he did not find the beloved person for whom he searched, his eyes turned to the distant, alluring mountains, with their remembered promise of endless space and freedom. After another fruitless course around the knoll, Tawny started for the mountains at a fast run.

He never knew that Charles Northcott and John Weston searched for him until the desert day ended and the sudden desert night fell like a lowering curtain over the greasewood and cactus. He never saw them finally walk back to the car, nor heard Charles Northcott say, "You were right, John. He did have a bronco streak."

"It will show up every time," Weston replied. There was passionate sympathy in his voice when he turned for one last look at the desert, for he knew what a dog could face there.

"Poor devil," he said. "He doesn't stand a chance. I hope he dies quickly."

3. The Desert

Tawny walked slowly, head down, jaws gaping, tongue lolling. When a pebble rattled, he swerved aside to investigate. But it was only a ground squirrel that, surprised away from its den, had scurried to get back into it. Tawny closed his jaws twice and resumed panting.

He looked toward the Lost Angels Mountains. Shimmering in the distance, tantalizingly near and yet so very far away, they were the lure that drew him, the place he wanted to reach. But he was finding obstacles in the way. He had left the two men hours ago, and traveled miles, but in all that distance there had not been so much as a trace of water. He was thirstier than he had ever been before.

Kennel-born and reared, Tawny had always had everything he needed provided for him. Never once had he had to exert himself for the necessities of life, and now he did not know how. But in spite of thirst so acute that it was almost torture, he did not panic.

He searched the desert with his eyes. There was little to distinguish this terrain from that over which he had been traveling; it was rocky land upon which grew cactus, greasewood, a few palo verde trees and, up on a knoll, a single joshua tree. A hundred feet away a quick-legged road runner scooted from one copse of cactus to another, and near it a covey of crested desert quail scratched busily about.

Beyond a passing glance, Tawny paid no attention. He needed water too badly even to think of food.

A little breeze sprang up and a single lonesome cloud drifted into the sky. Off in the distance began a discordant creaking that increased and decreased in both volume and cadence as the wind freshened or ebbed. Tawny looked toward the sound, but he had never before heard anything like it and was unable to identify it. He stored it away in his mind as something to be investigated when the opportunity presented.

Then, in the muted growl of a car, he heard a sound that he did know. Marking it, Tawny rose and started toward it. Cars meant human beings, and humans, in Tawny's experience, always had an ample store of everything. If he could find the car, he would also find water. The dog broke into a tired run.

The single cloud became a whole covey of clouds that presently joined forces and cast the desert in shadow. The wind blew in short, choppy gusts and the creaking noise became both louder and nearer. Tawny breasted a little rise and discovered its source.

Below him was a level space. In sharp contrast to the surrounding drab desert, here was a patch of bright green grass, a willow tree, and a grapefruit tree which bore both ripe fruit and heavy-scented blossoms. Four red-and-white cattle, too listless to move, stood under the tree, chewing placid cuds.

Fifty feet from them stood a windmill whose metal blades were turning in the breeze and whose unoiled axle was responsible for the creaking sound. As the blades turned, they pumped water into a metal tank that had once been bright and gleaming but was now so sun-scorched that it had turned dull grey. It was a stock tank put here by some optimist who had found a shallow water table and who, not knowing the desert, had thought that there would always be enough wind to turn the blades and keep the tank filled.

But there was water in the tank now. Tawny smelled it and broke into a run. The cattle looked quickly around, undecided for a moment whether to flee or stay. Seeing no threat in the running dog, they resumed chewing their cuds and switching their tails. Tawny reared against the tank to drink his fill. Then, climbing all the way in, he enjoyed a refreshing swim. Finally satisfied, he leaped out and shook himself.

Approaching the tank, he had come much nearer the road, and now heard another car go past. The only road leading into the Lost Angels, it was used mostly by those ranchers who lived in the country, or by occasional tourists. Tawny came to the road and halted.

He was bewildered, a little uncertain, and for the first time in his life, more than a little lonely. Never in his memory had he been without company of some kind, and he missed it now. If a car had come along just at that moment, and if the driver had stopped and called to him, Tawny would have welcomed human companionship. But no car came and Tawny plunged into the desert on the other side of the road.

His thirst quenched, hunger now made itself felt. But he was still bewildered and had had little time to adjust himself to these changed conditions. So when he ran at a jack rabbit, it eluded him. Panting, Tawny abandoned the chase and looked about. Then his eyes were attracted by a wheeling buzzard.

He didn't know what it was and, aside from the fact that it was soaring in effortless circles, he hadn't the slightest notion as to what it was doing. But the buzzard's circular flight intrigued the dog, and he trotted closer the better to see. He found the buzzard wheeling over a mountain lion kill, a fawn that had been pulled down the night before, partly eaten, and covered with pebbles and greasewood. Tawny scraped the twigs and stones aside and ate his fill. When the buzzard soared lower he growled savagely at it.

With night, Tawny lay up under a ledge of rock not far from the remains of the fawn. If it was not the best food he had ever eaten, it was food and he intended to stay by it. Tawny slept lightly, a part of his senses always alert, and came completely awake when a pebble rattled.

With his fast reflexes, he was ready for action the instant he awakened, but he wanted to identify whatever was coming before he decided what to do about it. His nostrils were filled with a strong but not unpleasant odor; the lion that had killed the fawn was coming back to get it. Protecting what he considered had now become his, Tawny roared to the attack.

At once the lion wheeled and fled. Wanting only to guard his food cache, Tawny did not follow. But the incident gave him a sense of confidence. He was alone in the desert, but he was learning to get along.

Tawny did not go back to sleep beneath the rock ledge for he was thirsty again. The only water he knew was in the tank where he had stopped the previous afternoon. But to go there would mean to leave the fawn, his only food supply. Then the problem was solved for him.

The cloud banks that had been gathering turned inside out and the rain sluiced down. It was not a gentle storm, for little about the desert is gentle. The rain fell as though it had to offer in a short time enough water to keep the desert alive for months. Rivers of sand flowed water once again. Floods surged down dry washes. With only short lulls, the rain poured down for two days and two nights. Aside from bringing water to a parched land, it took away Tawny's last link with civilization. The rain washed the road out and for three days after the storm, nobody at all traveled it.

When his food was gone and Tawny decided to travel again, his way led him into the desert. He started at night, traveled steadily, and when the morning sun rose, he was far back. Standing on the side of a little hill, he looked around.

A veritable forest of saguaro marched away in disorderly lines, and mingled with it was the usual greasewood, various other varieties of cacti, palo verde trees, some ironwoods, and a grove of mesquite whose branches were tangled with mistletoe. It was wild country seldom seen by humans because few had the hardihood to venture into it. But it was not devoid of life.

Attracted by erratic motion, Tawny's questing gaze fastened on a medium-sized beast that was rushing furiously about. Eighteen inches tall by three feet long, the creature weighed about twenty-five pounds. It was covered with grizzled-grey bristles and there was a white band around its neck. Its small-eared head ended in a tusked snout. It was a javelina, or peccary, a pig-like wild beast that is not a pig at all.

The javelina scraped the earth with its hoofed feet, making ready to rush again. Then Tawny saw that it was fighting a big rattlesnake.

Beneath a sprig of greasewood, the rattler's body lay in fat coils. In almost the exact center of the coiled mass, grey rattles whirred their warning. Its head was erect, beads of eyes fixed on the javelina.

Every bristle erect, so that it appeared a full third bigger than it actually was, the javelina launched another charge. Just outside the range that the rattler's striking head was able to reach, it stopped short. The snake's head flicked forward and for a second it lay uncoiled. It was the chance for which the javelina had been waiting. As though made of rubber, it bounced into the air and came down with all four hoofs scraping furiously. Sliced to bits, the snake's body trembled and its jaws gaped.

Instinctively Tawny launched his own charge at the javelina and saw it wheel and flee before him. Sure that this relatively slow beast was no match for him, Tawny closed the gap between them. Suddenly a hot pain sliced his right shoulder and a blow sent him tumbling over on his left side. But his was a greyhound's agility and his reflexes were conditioned to the track. Instead of floundering helplessly, he rolled over a second time and was on his feet again. Almost too late, he saw his error.

Pursued, the snake-killing javelina had sought a nearby herd of its companions and now, sixteen strong, they were on all sides. The one whose tusks had ripped Tawny came in for a second attack, snorted, and stopped, bristling. The javelinas' little eyes flamed and their ivory tusks snapped in discordant cadence as they closed in for the kill. Tawny danced nervously, wanting only to escape.

There was no escape, no hole through which he could slip. As soon as Tawny realized that, he did the only thing he could do, and attacked.

He charged swiftly, snarling and bristling. The young boar against which he launched himself would have fought to a finish had its fellows attacked Tawny. But the herd scattered and the young boar would not stand alone. It broke and ran.

Tawny ran alongside, slashing as he did so, for his anger had risen to a hot peak. He disliked to be cornered, and he would revenge himself if he could. Finally the young boar turned, backed weakly against a boulder, and tried to defend itself. It was too far gone, and a moment later Tawny pulled it down. He ate and liked the musky flesh.

That night Tawny went back to the road some four miles from the place where he had first crossed it. He found and sniffed at a dead dog lying near a clump of cholla and slunk away, bristling. The dog, abandoned on the lonely desert road, had suffered a slow and dreadful death. Knowing nothing of this, Tawny sensed only that there was something terrible about this body of one of his own kind. All night long he traveled back into the desert; he had lost all desire to visit the road.

Seared by an unseasonably hot sun, the puddles left by the rain dried up, the rivers flowed sand again, and Tawny must once more cast for water. But his thirst was not quite so tormenting this time; he was adjusting fast to desert life.

Late that afternoon he found the water hole. It was only a little trickle that flowed out of the sand, formed a pool thirty feet long by six wide, and fed its overflow back into the sand. But the area it affected was amazingly different from the rest of the desert.

Great cottonwoods sent deep roots into the watered earth. Willows grew beside the water, and a profusion of lesser brush. There was a rich carpet of green grass that furnished food for a horde of desert cottontails. Tawny drank deeply and looked with great interest at the swarm of tiny fish that swam in this shaded pool. They were Gambusia-minnows, or mosquito fish. Miles from any other surface water, with only desert in between, there was no accounting for their presence. But they were here.

That day and that night Tawny learned what water means to desert dwellers.

This water hole was a Mecca for wild life from miles around. In the late afternoon flocks of doves appeared, drank, and winged back to their nests. Next came the Gambel quail, flocks of anywhere from five to thirty, their topknots bobbing and their voices filling the air as old friends greeted each other. When the sun dipped toward the west, the scrawny cattle that ranged the area trooped in for their daily drink.

In the desert there is no real twilight, but only a short grey period that is neither completely light nor completely dark. The first of the mule deer came then. A big buck that had shed its antlers and sprouted knobs of new ones, drank its fill, tossed its head, and gave itself over to grazing on the green grass. The buck was followed by a herd of nine wild burros. Tough and wiry little beasts, they politely lined up beside each other and drank. Then came more deer, and while they were drinking, two bobcats peacefully drank from the other side of the water hole. But when a tough old boar led in a big herd of javelina, the bobcats and deer maintained a respectful distance while the javelina were at the water hole. Only the tail-switching burros regarded them complacently.

The javelina started back to the heights from which they had come, and a grey fox padded in for his drink. The big buck deer, having grazed his fill and feeling suddenly playful, bounced stiff-leggedly at the fox. The fox ducked behind a clump of cactus and the buck struck at him again. For five minutes, until tired of it, the buck amused himself teasing the fox.

Save for that, and it was really play, there was not the faintest show of hostility. Many of the creatures that watered here were enemies. Yet it was as though the water hole, which sustained life in all, was a place of truce.

In the dim light of early morning, even the mountain sheep that lived in the surrounding heights came down.

Led by an old matriarch, a herd of eleven ewes and lambs quenched their thirst. After them came seven curly-horned rams.

The run rose, but before the desert was given over to a hot day, Tawny ran down a jack rabbit for his breakfast. He was learning. This life suited him, and if he was lonely, he was free.

He stopped on a ridge and looked north. Almost ten thousand feet above sea level, the cloud-piercing peaks of the Lost Angels were etched like blue shadows against the sky. Tawny stared at them for a long while, and then went on.

When his path was blocked by a squat, chubby lizard about fourteen inches long he halted a second time. The reptile's body was whitish, tinged with red, and dark stripes encircled its body. Its scaly front feet were planted in a dove's nest. It regarded Tawny with cold eyes and continued swallowing an egg while the distressed dove fluttered in a nearby mesquite.

Tawny circled, knowing instinctively that the lizard was better let alone. It was a Gila monster, a forked-tongue lizard so venomous that men have died from its bite. But it was a sluggish thing that could easily be avoided. Farther on, Tawny circled again when a thick-bodied rattlesnake sounded its warning.

Sheerly by accident, he strayed into a clump of jumping cactus and before he could back up, all four paws were pierced by pods that had become detached from the main stems. Finding a clear space, Tawny lay down to bite the pods from his feet and spit them out. But he could not extract all the hairthin spines, and the acid with which they were tipped made his feet burn. Obviously it paid to be careful when he walked, and he marked the jumping cactus as something to be avoided in the future.

He became thirsty, and had there been water he would have drunk. But his was not the agonizing thirst that another breed of dog in similar circumstances might have felt. Tawny's remote ancestors had been tamed by desert men, and had learned of necessity to endure thirst. In part, Tawny had inherited that ability.

Two hours after leaving the first one, he found another water hole and knew it at once because of the trees and brush. Tawny drank, rested, and watched the approach of evening bring desert dwellers out of the various hunting or grazing grounds where they had spent the day.

Restless, with growing confidence in his own powers and possessing both strength and endurance, Tawny ranged where he wished to go. He found all five of the water holes in the immediate area. High in the sun-baked rocky hills, where wild sheep had their lonely pastures and almost nothing else ventured, he discovered a sixth.

Here a mountain of rock rose for six hundred feet, but it was not solid rock. Seamed with cracks and fissures, it offered seepage for the water that fell during storms. When the sun blazed again, this water was protected by an insulation of rock so thick that it could not evaporate. Deep within the mountain were subterranean reservoirs. Their outlet was in a shaded little cave in the mountain's side. Within the cave there were always from three to eight inches of clear, cold water. But there was never any outside because whatever flowed out was blotted up by the sun.

Food became no problem because of the countless jack rabbits. It was five minutes' work to find one, and should that one elude him by dodging into a dry wash or cactus thicket where he could no longer see it, another could soon be found. But Tawny varied his fare.

With his lightning speed he could catch deer. Though the adult bucks and does were too much for him to handle by himself, twice he pulled down fawns. Bobcats, surprised more than a few jumps from a palo verde, ironwood, or saguaro into which they could climb, were easily overtaken and not hard to kill. Herds of javelina were dangerous and almost invincible, but many herds could be broken, enabling Tawny to kill lone stragglers. Of all desert dwellers, only the pronghorn antelope could outrun Tawny.

He became whip-hard and steadily continued to learn.

He knew where the scaly rattlesnakes hunted and where they lay up. He knew the routes of the Gila monsters. He saw for himself how the pack rats made their homes all but unassailable by heaping them high with cactus thorns. He knew where the jack rabbits and cottontails played and where each was most abundant. He was acquainted with every scrawny cow that nibbled a livelihood out of the desert. He was aware of the drinking times of various animals and the water hole favored by each. He taught himself to lie up during the noon heat and to range in the early morning, evening, or at night.

And he acquired an intense hatred of coyotes.

It began when Tawny found a javelina one nightfall. This was a yearling boar that had been driven out by the old herd boar and that had as yet been unable to acquire a harem of its own. Tawny attacked instantly.

Had the young boar backed against a rock and defended itself, Tawny would have been forced to wear it down by rushing and feinting, and that was dangerous. A javelina's tusks can inflict serious wounds, and the wild desert pigs are agile. But instead of standing to fight, this boar chose a running battle.

Tawny ran alongside. He sliced as he ran, and every

time his teeth cut the javelina, the boar turned to strike back. When it did, Tawny dodged and returned to strike again. The little boar was amazingly tough. It finally turned at bay on the rim of a ledge of rock that dropped sheer into a narrow canyon. Weakened at last, it fell from the ledge.

Tawny balanced on the rim, peering into the darkness and waiting for the boar to strike on the boulders below. As soon as he heard the boar land, Tawny began to run. He knew the canyon, and the way into it. He raced to the nearest sloping cleft, descended it, and made his way back to where the javelina had fallen. A fierce snarl rippled from his throat.

A whole pack of coyotes had gotten there before him and had made the most of the opportunity. There was nothing left of the javelina save a few spots of blood, a few splintered bones, and scattered strips of tough hide. From then on, Tawny declared war on all coyotes, evolving his own technique for dealing with them.

He discovered that most coyotes, closely pursued, turned to fight. But they turned only as a last resort and would always run again if a way was opened. Tawny learned to lunge and then to withdraw. Without exception, the little desert wolves would run again, and so doing, give way to near panic. Tawny had only to close in from the side, set his powerful jaws on the coyote's neck, and throw his enemy. The coyotes that did not break their necks, when they tumbled end over end, were easily dealt with before they could get up.

Tawny went where he pleased and did as he wished, but so doing brought him afoul of trouble.

4. Wild Pack

Brutus, the leader of the wild pack, was a lean Alsatian. In any other circumstances he would have been not only a good, but an exceptional dog, for his was a high order of intelligence. Brutus was an outlaw only because thoughtless people had made him one, and his story was almost the story of the entire pack.

Every autumn, when icy winds blew and snow fell in northern climates, thousands of people turned to the desert. One such family bought Brutus, at the time a cuddly, two-month-old puppy, to serve as a playmate for its two children. The family stayed the winter through, and Brutus grew up with it, perfectly contented.

Then spring came. For the family, spring meant a return to its northern home. For Brutus it meant exile. No longer a playful puppy but a good-sized dog, he was too large to be taken in the car. Nor was there anyone to offer him a home. There was a dog pound where Brutus could have had a quick and merciful death. Instead of consigning Brutus to it, the kinder way, his master drove him into the Lost Angels, and left him there. The master salved his conscience by assuring himself that Brutus would find his way to a ranch or homestead and have a fine home. It never occurred to him that the nearest ranch was twenty miles away, or that every rancher who would take in these discarded waifs already had as many as he could keep. Not once did he even imagine that he was consigning the dog to almost sure death on the desert.

For a while after he had been abandoned, Brutus interested himself in snuffling about. Then he grew lonely, and when another car traveled the road he met it eagerly. But it did not stop for him. Puzzled, Brutus waited patiently, with no idea that he had been abandoned. Furthermore, he hadn't the faintest notion as to how to take care of himself. For hours, supremely confident that his master would return, he waited hopefully within a hundred feet of the road. Thirst tormented him and he made a few little forays to look for water, which he did not find. At nightfall his misery was increased by a sense of desolation.

Never in his life had he been alone, and he was desperately afraid of loneliness. Any human at all would have been welcome, and when none came Brutus tagged forlornly after a scrawny old cow that crossed the road with a calf at her heels. When Brutus came too near, the cow shook threatening horns. But she did not mind if he maintained his distance, and to the lonely dog anything was better than being deserted. Staggering, enduring awful thirst, he kept the cow and calf in sight only because his fear of being alone drove him along.

Brutus was delirious with thirst when the cow finally led him to the water hole from which she and the calf drank every night at this time. Brutus drank his fill and did not move again until dawn. The cow and calf were gone and again he was lonely. But, though he knew how to get back to the road, he feared to leave the water hole. Still, he must eat.

That first day he filled his stomach with green grass, retched it all up again, and spent a miserably sick night. But the next day, still not daring to get out of sight of water, he found and ate a fledgling dove that had fallen from its nest. That night, while he lay all alone, a cottontail ventured almost up to him. Brutus had only to lunge to catch it.

Not a trailing dog, depending on his eyes and ears as much as his nose, Brutus learned where young quail peeped about their mothers and found that he could catch them. He discovered that young doves unable to fly often fell out of their crude nests in palo verde trees and cottonwoods. Not fast enough to catch jack rabbits, Brutus learned to ambush them.

It was not a rich livelihood. It did sustain life, but Brutus became gaunt as summer lengthened and fierce heat lay like a solid blanket all day long. Often the heat lessened only a little with nightfall, though it was always a blessing to be out of the sun. But that burning summer, the desert's fiercest time, taught Brutus how to survive. He became wiser, and in a few short months discovered things which in other circumstances he might not have learned in a lifetime. Though he still ate skimpily and sporadically, and found much of his food by watching buzzards and taking for himself whatever they located, he developed the urge and the experience to branch out. But it was not until October that his desert way of life sharply changed.

One day he came upon an antelope with a broken leg. It was a big buck and Brutus halted, inborn caution bidding him be careful before he rushed in. He had caught rabbits and chased bigger game, but he had never pulled down anything as large as an antelope.

Seeing the dog, the buck ran. It was fleet in spite of the broken leg, and for a while lengthened the distance between them. But it was no longer equal to a hard and sustained flight, and finally turned at bay, its rear against a boulder. Its head was down, threatening antlers presented as Brutus rushed in.

Had the buck been unhurt, Brutus might have been seriously injured and perhaps killed. As it was, the buck was seriously handicapped by its broken leg, and was able to strike just hard enough to roll him over.

Brutus got up, his prudence restored by the blow. He wanted to kill the buck, but not get himself hurt in so doing. He might have left the field to the still-agile buck had there not been an interruption caused by another dog.

This was a bristled airedale named Rowdy. Like Brutus, he was another unwanted dog that had been turned loose on the desert when his presence became a problem. Rowdy had spent the summer at another water hole, from which he had recently been driven by a herd of javelina. He had sighted the injured buck from a pinnacle, sensed that it would be easy prey, and now came rushing in to get it himself.

When the buck turned to face Rowdy, Brutus saw his chance. Rushing in, he slashed at the buck's neck. That and the full impact of Brutus' weight toppled the crippled beast. For a moment the buck kicked its three good legs wildly, breaking its own neck in the struggle. Instinct drove both dogs to its throat, and the antelope was dead in seconds.

For a short interval both dogs stood stiff-legged and bristling. Each had had a part in the kill and each could claim the buck. But in each was a great loneliness that attracted one to the other. Instead of fighting, they sniffed noses, wagged tails and side by side fell to feeding.

After that they traveled together, and made a good team. Of the dogs cast loose every year, few lived more than a week. Those that survived were the resourceful, superior animals with above-average intelligence or strength and more than their share of luck. Now, to the advantage of both, Rowdy and Brutus combined their talents, although Brutus was the leader.

Ferocious enough, Rowdy was almost wholly a creature of impulse. Finding something that showed fight, his first reaction was to fight it, and he joined every battle that offered. His body was covered with scars and recent wounds. The javelina that had driven Rowdy from his water hole would have killed him if, just as the fight was waxing hottest, a piglet following the herd had not become wedged in a crevice, causing the rest to turn back to help the young one. For once in his life exercising prudence, Rowdy had run on. But, rather than teach him any lasting judgment, the incident had done little save create a burning hatred of all javelina.

Both dogs had been restricted before because of the need for water. Now their range was considerably expanded, for Rowdy knew one water hole and Brutus another, and it was only about four hours' travel between the two. All the country between was made available to them.

Brutus taught Rowdy how to find food by watching buzzards. They waylaid jack rabbits and between them caught and pulled down a calf that had become separated from its mother. This was a feat that neither had been capable of before, and it gave them an increasing sense of their combined power. This was further developed when they met the herd of javelina that had routed Rowdy.

Led by a sour-tempered old sow, the herd of thirteen wild pigs was busily devouring the spined pads of prickly pear when the two dogs happened upon them. The old sow grunted and whirled, and the seven other adults in the herd closed ranks beside her. The piglets huddled behind their elders, and for a moment the opposing forces faced each other.

Rowdy snarled fiercely and leaped stiff-leggedly to a frontal attack. Brutus knew better. His was an instinctive generalship, and he sensed immediately that the weakness of the javelina lay in the piglets. While the adults faced Rowdy, Brutus circled and slashed, killing a piglet. At once the adults turned to charge, giving Rowdy his opportunity. He raced behind, nipping at their haunches. The wild pigs whirled on Rowdy and Brutus got another piglet.

Disorganized, the javelina fled, running on short legs into the cactus while both dogs chivvied them on and pulled down still another piglet. Then the dogs returned to the feast made possible by their combined efforts.

A month later, Joey joined their ranks.

Together, Rowdy and Brutus were faring much better than either had alone. But though both used their noses, neither had mastered the finer points of trailing game. They could stalk and they could rush, but should whatever they hunted get out of sight, they did not know how to find it again.

They were prowling a boulder-strewn ridge that overlooked a tangle of cholla cactus when they first saw Joey. Nose to the ground and ears flapping, he was trailing up a dry wash. Suddenly a fawn that neither had known was there burst out of the cactus and in its precipitate flight almost overran Brutus and Rowdy. They had only to close in, one from either side, and pull it down.

Joey was the only member of the wild pack who was not an outcast. A little fourteen-inch beagle, he had been the pride and joy of a hunter who had bought him because Joey had a seeming invulnerability to the cactus that proved the downfall of so many other hunting dogs. It was the owner's fond hope that Joey would hunt rabbits, but Joey had more of a liking for deer scent. He also had a wild streak. So instead of returning to the master who awaited him, Joey was happy to stay with Brutus and Rowdy.

In the middle of the winter they were joined by two more outcasts. Bull, a pit bull, and Major, a big cur, had separated a wild burro from its herd and were attacking it when Brutus, Rowdy, and Joey arrived on the scene to help.

They became a tightly knit, efficient, savage machine that depended on Joey's nose, Rowdy's, Bull's and Major's strength, and Brutus' brains. As their knowledge of the country grew, they ranged throughout the desert and into the highest parts of the Lost Angels. They feared nothing for nothing could stand before them. Even the herds of javelina fled when the wild pack came. They knew all the water holes, every game trail, and became undisputed masters of the area.

They lost Major one day when they were high in the Lost Angels, and there did a deed that, had it become known, would have brought about the death of the whole pack.

Joey was coursing a deer and the rest were following along when a shot rang out. Joey stopped, for he knew what a gunshot meant. Then he surged ahead, the rest following.

In the pine forest they came upon an old prospector. Rifle in hand, he was bending over the deer that the wild pack had marked for its own. True to his impulsive nature, Rowdy rushed on, Major beside him. Looking up, the startled prospector had just time enough to rise and shoot once more. His bullet caught Major squarely in the heart. Incensed by the death of one of their members, hot with the chase and grown savage by their wild life, the rest of the pack surged forward. The old prospector was left beside Major.

Nothing ever came of it, but the incident taught the pack caution. It also wiped out the last bond with man. The pack no longer felt human ties, but only realized that men had it in their power to strike back—the only creatures that could hurt them. A week later, the pack replaced the dead Major with Pal, a big pointer that some city dweller had given to the desert.

Though often Brutus bent himself to suit circumstance or circumstance to suit himself, he developed one inflexible rule. No other dog must be tolerated in any part of the range that the pack had marked for its own. If one was found there, it was killed as swiftly as possible.

Most of these summary lynchings were blessings in disguise, for almost without exception the dogs found by the wild pack were outcasts that had been abandoned. Sooner or later almost all of them would have died anyhow, but not nearly as swiftly as they did at the fangs of the pack.

That was the situation when they first came upon Tawny. Brutus in the lead and Joey trailing yards in the rear, they strung out after the strange grey-hound.

TAWNY's scent was relatively dull. But his eyes missed little and he saw the wild dogs as soon as they broke from cover. For the fractional part of a second, Tawny stayed where he was.

He did not see the wild pack as any other dog would have seen them; to Tawny they were more than just five running animals. Keen eyes were a part of Tawny's heritage, and life in the desert had sharpened his perception. Therefore, he noted the individual characteristics of each dog in the pack and by the time he turned to run he had a fair idea of each one's speed.

Anger flared as he ran, for his was fighting blood, too. But it was balanced by a generous measure of common sense. Rowdy, seeing five dogs coming at him, might have met them all. Tawny knew that he had no chance against the pack, so he ran. However, he had no intention of running any faster than was necessary, and it was not necessary to run full speed. Tawny turned at right angles to the course he had been following so that, without slackening pace, he could look at the wild pack and see what it was doing.

Brutus, the fastest dog in the pack, was a good five lengths ahead, followed by Pal. Striving to keep up, but lacking the speed to do so, Rowdy was next, with Bull half a jump behind him. Joey, steadily losing ground, was twenty yards in the rear.

When Tawny changed his angle of flight, the fast-thinking Brutus cut across the hypotenuse of the triangle and managed to close the distance between them by seven yards. It was a wise move, one Brutus had often used to bring himself closer to fleeing deer. But Tawny was unworried. If he cared to use all his speed, he could leave this whole straining pack of comparatively slow dogs far behind. But he wanted to cut back and go in the direction he had been traveling when the pack cut him off. There was a water hole a few ridges over and he was thirsty.

At the same time, his anger did not lessen. He would not have joined the wild dogs anyway, but he resented being driven. A proud dog, he had the heart and courage of greyhounds once bred for the sole purpose of catching and holding dangerous game, and his intelligence fully equalled Brutus'. He was not going to leave the pack without teaching them that he could fight. Deliberately Tawny slackened his pace.

When he did, Brutus redoubled his efforts. Brutus' life had made him hard as nails and constant ranging kept him that way. Always, when it was needed, he could summon extra speed and maintain a fast pace for far longer than any pampered domestic dog. He raced along with full confidence that he would soon pull this trespasser down and kill him.

That was exactly what Tawny wanted him to think, and when Brutus was only two jumps behind, Tawny whirled suddenly. He had learned his running on the greyhound track where a twist, a bend, or an ability to see an opening, often meant a telling difference. The move was wholly unanticipated. When Brutus' own momentum carried him past, Tawny struck. His slicing teeth cut Brutus' flank and Tawny leaped away again. But he had underestimated his enemy.

Naturally fast, Brutus had behind him all the experience brought about by a hundred fights with deer, javelina, wild burros, bobcats, and once, with a young lion that the pack had surprised on the ground. He was a master of slashing and parrying and he was faster than a coyote. Brutus aimed for Tawny's neck, just missed, and cleanly slashed Tawny's leather collar. But when he followed up to press his attack, Tawny wasn't there.

He had leaped clear over Brutus and hit the earth running. A smoke-colored streak, he circled the furious Rowdy and Bull because they were too close together and he knew better than to face two dogs. Tawny flashed in beside Pal, struck, and heard a shrill yelp of pain as Pal rolled away from him.

With no time for a real fight, Tawny's slash had merely grazed Brutus' skin and left a slight gash in Pal's side. But it had taught Brutus. Few of the dogs that the wild pack destroyed showed fight. When found, more than half were too far gone to fight, and the rest usually tried to appease the killers. None had lasted more than a minute. Obviously Tawny was neither weak nor craven. He merited respect and caution. Though Brutus

might have outdistanced Rowdy and Bull, Brutus
suited his pace to theirs. Should Tawny turn again,
there would be at least three of the wild pack to oppose
him.

Tawny had no intention of turning. Already thirsty,
the run had made him doubly so and his dangling
tongue was hot and dry. He lengthened out leaving the
wild pack far behind, and made his way toward the
water hole. Nothing except game that he wanted to
catch could make him use that furious pace which,
afterwards, left him so exhausted that he must sleep for
hours. Now Tawny traveled at a natural gait, one that he
could maintain for as long as necessary, but it was still
fast enough to outdistance the pack.

When he could no longer see the wild dogs, Tawny
slowed to a walk.

He stopped to bite a cactus burr out of his paw, then
padded happily across the cool green grass surrounding
the water hole. He drank deeply, lifted his head to let
water spatter from his jaws back into the water hole, and
drank again. He looked about him.

In this hottest part of the day, quail huddled in their
cactus thickets and rabbits stretched in whatever shade
was available. There was little motion, and because his
nose was not attuned to the various living creatures
near him, Tawny did not know they were there. He
drank a little more and looked back to see if the wild
dogs were coming. When he did not see them, he
stretched full length in the green grass.

Tawny was not hungry for he had eaten earlier. He
was a bit lonely, but not so distressingly alone that he
thought of returning to Charles Northcott. There was no
man to whom he owed loyalty and none to whom he
would go. Once he had belonged to Fred Haver. Now
he belonged only to himself, and Tawny preferred it
that way.

A half hour later, the wild pack came again.

Led by the keen-nosed, trail-snuffling Joey, they came filing down the rocky knob that Tawny himself had descended. Since, on this heat-ridden day, scent lay poorly and the wild dogs' pace was necessarily limited to Joey's, they were not coming fast.

Tawny got up, slipped uneasily through the cottonwoods, climbed the ridge on the other side, and turned to watch. He had no liking for the wild dogs, but neither did he have any real quarrel with them. Left alone, he would gladly leave them alone. However, though he did know uneasiness, at no time did he feel any fear. He had already proven his ability to run away from the wild dogs, and if it came to a fight he would fight them. Now he waited to see what they were going to do. When he saw Joey come through the cottonwoods and start up the ridge on which he sat, Tawny climbed to the ridge's summit and ran swiftly along it to another water hole.

An hour after dark, the wild pack found him again.

Tawny could not see clearly, but he heard. He sprang to his feet, angered. He wanted no fight and would avoid one if he could. But he did not care to be hunted.

He met the wild dogs on the carpet of green grass, and dodged aside when all five rushed as one. He circled, waiting for one of the five to break ranks. It was the fierce Bull that finally bounced stiffly toward him. Tawny waited, as though he intended to meet his enemy head on, then he slipped to one side, and his teeth sliced flesh. Tawny rippled away from Bull.

Brutus led the wild pack partly because he was the strongest but largely because he could think better and faster than any of the others. As he took the measure of everything he fought, so he took Tawny's measure. Brutus was ready when Bull bounced out, and launched his own attack. The greyhound dodged with such dazzling speed that Brutus missed the paunch at which he had aimed with the intention of disemboweling his enemy. Instead, he succeeded only in leaving a gaping wound on Tawny's hip. Then the greyhound was gone into the darkness.

Tawny's anger mounted. Seeking no quarrel, he would nevertheless accept one that had been forced upon him. However, though he thought himself a match for any one member of the wild pack, he sensed that it would be sheer suicide to fight them all. Tawny traveled back toward the other water hole, only to find the wild dogs upon him again in the grey dawn.

For a whole week, never daring to rest for very long and always faced with the necessity of watching and listening for the wild dogs, Tawny fled before them. Again he fought with Rowdy, Bull, and Pal. Once, before the little beagle managed to yelp back to the pack's protection, he slashed Joey's long ear. But he could never break the pack for very long and the fights never lasted for more than a hit and run encounter. Had Tawny lingered with his antagonist of the moment, the rest of the pack would have overwhelmed him.

Then the wild pack came no more.

Tawny could not know that they had a set way of life, or that they passed only the winters in the desert. When summer came, they climbed into the high peaks, where it was always cool. Furthermore, numbers of wild sheep and male deer sought the high country in summer, so that during the hot months the peaks offered the best hunting.

One blazing day when he did not feel like resting, Tawny was descending the nose of a low ridge when, looking across the gully below him, he saw a coyote sitting on the opposite ridge. The animal's tail was flat behind him. Pointed ears were erect and mouth parted as, with vast interest, the coyote studied something that only he could see.

Tawny began to slink. Since he ran by sight, he could course only what he was able to see. The coyote was over a hundred yards away, and should Tawny start to run now, it would almost certainly get out of sight. The greyhound had narrowed the distance between them to about fifty yards when the coyote saw him and flicked away. Tawny lengthened out to run. He gained the opposite ridge, saw the coyote streaking through the cactus ahead of him, and was about to continue the chase when he halted in his tracks. Looking into a dry wash, he saw what the coyote had been studying with such fascination.

It was a fluffy, four-months-old collie pup, a tri-color with a black, gold, and white coat. An aristocratic muzzle and good lines betrayed fine breeding, but the pup was another outcast for all of that. Named Sable, for his black saddle, he had been loosed in the desert by an owner who no longer wanted a collie pup.

Sable's jaws gaped wide and his dangling tongue lolled full length. In desperate need of water, he had come this far from the road without finding any.

For a moment Tawny stood indecisively, then loneliness sent him forward. Wagging an appeasing tail, the young collie advanced to meet him. They sniffed noses and Sable whined. Tawny sniffed his newfound companion from head to foot, made a playful little rush, and Sable snapped playfully back. When Tawny turned to leave, Sable followed.

Tawny did not deliberately lead him toward water; he did not reason that much. But he wanted water himself, and when he started into the desert, it was toward a water hole. The collie did his valiant best to keep up and couldn't do it. Not wanting to lose a friend now that he'd found one, Tawny waited. He sniffed Sable again and resumed the journey.

But the sun was merciless and Sable wouldn't have

made it had not a thirsty range cow been this way only a short time before. A long way from the water herself, she had used her hoofs to break apart a squat barrel cactus. Shaped somewhat like a keg, its roots scarcely bigger than a cabbage's, the barrel cactus was its own reservoir. Its insides were a mass of pulpy cells and there, during the few times when it did rain, the barrel cactus stored water to last throughout the scorching months when it did not. Recently shattered, its pulpy segments still oozed moisture.

Tawny gulped a piece, and Sable imitated him. Eagerly he sought another chunk of pulp, and when a hooked spine penetrated his downy fur and pierced his leg, he merely whined and gulped some more. It was not tasty, but it was water. He could go on now.

Completely trusting, glad enough to have older shoulders to bear his burdens, Sable padded at Tawny's heels. When they finally came in sight of the water hole, a coyote flashed away. While Tawny leaped in pursuit, Sable sat where he was and watched.

The coyote, a young one, did not turn at bay, so Tawny called on all his speed, and drew up beside his enemy. He struck, threw the coyote end over end, and was upon it before it could get up. Tawny clenched both jaws around the coyote's neck, shook it until it moved no more, then started back to Sable.

Up on a ridge, about three hundred yards away, a young rancher named Dick Hartson witnessed the chase from beginning to end.

5. Dick Hartson

Although Dick Hartson had been born and brought up in the shadow of the Lost Angels, he had been away from the desert for the past three years.

First had come his military service. He had not resented Army life, but neither had he liked it. Too often, in some distant barracks, he had awakened to dream of purple hills at sundown, or blazing golden ones at sunrise. Even in an Army kitchen the pungent odor of greasewood had never left his nostrils. His service career had been a duty and was something to be remembered. But unless there was another war, it was not something he wanted to repeat.

After his discharge, he had tried life in the city, sure that it would be both colorful and fascinating. For awhile, because it was all new and fresh, city life had been exciting. Then had come unrest. His room, though comfortable, was one of a thousand that had been stamped out of exactly the same pattern. The restaurants where he ate his meals were interesting at first, but after three months they assumed a strangely similar pattern, too. The seventy-five dollars a week he earned in the factory where he worked did not seem nearly as much in the city as he had expected they would.

As the months went by he discovered for himself that the lives most city dwellers lead are prosaic enough. He began to feel fettered and confined, and found himself thinking more and more about two periods of his life that stood out with increasing clarity. One was his earlier years in the desert. The other was the more recent time when, on an Army transport, he had shipped from a west-coast port to Hawaii. While at sea, he had been contented. The ocean was vast, wild, untamed. He had come to understand why so many sailors loved their calling and felt that he could be happy as a sailor. At the same time, he still dreamed of the Lost Angels and cactus in bloom, and felt the hot desert wind fan his cheek. In the end, the odor of the greasewood proved stronger than the tang of brine, and he decided to go back to the ranch.

He dropped off the train that brought him to the desert city at nine in the morning and boarded a bus that took him to the big produce market. At twenty past ten he climbed into the pickup truck of Manuel Gomez, who greeted Dick as though he had seen him yesterday instead of three years ago.

After the greetings, they drove largely in silence, for neither was a waster of words. When they passed the citrus groves and cotton fields, the part of the desert that had been tamed, and reached the greasewood and cactus that still defied encroaching civilization, Dick leaned eagerly forward in the seat. An hour after they left the city, he saw the sign still on its cottonwood post. The post leaned crazily, and the sign was weatherstained, but legible:

C-2 Ranch. 3 Miles

No fresh car tracks led toward the C-2. Dick's father, his only surviving relative, had died three months after he entered the service. Evidently nobody had visited the ranch in a long time. Manuel swerved toward the turn-off, but Dick stopped him.

"I left my saddle at Carlin's."

Manuel nodded understandingly. No true desert dweller ever sells his saddle no matter how badly he needs money, for if he has none how is he going to ride a horse over the countless acres into which no wheeled vehicle can go? Manuel drove on to Les Carlin's, and Les greeted Dick warmly.

"Glad to see you back, boy. I kept your saddle soaped; figgered you'd need it. Once you got alkali in your blood, you always come back to it."

"I guess so," Dick smiled.

Les also had a horse, a tough little camel-necked bay named Croppy. Croppy didn't like riders and he'd win no prizes for looks at even a second-rate horse show. But he was desert-bred, he could go without water as long as any horse, and he was a good buy for sixty dollars. Dick rode him until he stopped bucking, waved, and started back down the road.

He had-lingering doubts. He'd left an easy job that paid him seventy-five dollars a week, for a harsh desert where, at the present time, he was not at all sure that he could earn seventy-five a year. He stopped at the road leading to his ranch and braced the sign until it stood erect. That seemed symbolic. From now on the affairs of the C-2 were going to run straight.

A mile and a half from the main road, the dim tracks he'd been following faded into near-nothingness. Dick reined Croppy in on a little hillock and surveyed his kingdom.

The house, an adobe-brick structure, had been built so that a rising hill shaded it from the fierce rays of the afternoon sun. The rest of the ranch consisted of a pole corral, two weatherbeaten sheds, and fifteen hundred acres of greasewood, palo verdes, mesquite, cactus, grass, and rattlesnakes. Rising trees and lush vegetation revealed two water holes, and farther back there was another. Dick looped Croppy's reins over the top pole of the corral and went into the house.

Dust had settled thickly and pack rats scurried away, but nothing had apparently been disturbed by any human hand. Suddenly Dick's doubts melted and he felt completely at ease. He had come home, and a plan that had been vaguely forming for months began to take definite shape and structure in his mind.

Though Dick knew of none who had made fortunes, most sheep men did well enough. The bigger operators, those who ran three thousand or more sheep, grazed their flocks in rich alpine pastures during the summer and transported them, usually by rail, to the desert when winter came. Within sight of the C-2, with desert all around and the high peaks on the horizon, existed the same conditions that made these men prosperous. Sheep could be wintered on the desert and driven into the high country when summer came.

The fact that Dick hadn't any money with which to buy a flock of sheep was a minor point. He had left the desert just after his seventeenth birthday and was returning to it four months short of his twentieth. He was young, he knew he could earn money, and he didn't need three thousand sheep to start. If, perhaps even this year, he could manage to acquire a good ram and a few top-grade ewes, he was willing to build from there.

Dick scratched his head ruefully. He'd been so intrigued with the idea of returning home that he'd forgotten a few things, among them the fact that there would be nothing to eat in the house, and he'd neglected to bring anything. He might still mount Croppy and go down to Enos Blake's store, but that would mean an eight-mile ride and he didn't want to do that today. He'd rather eat jack rabbit.

Dick stripped Croppy's saddle, replaced his bridle with a halter, tied a thirty-foot picket rope to it, led him to the nearest water hole, and picketed him where he could reach both grass and water. Walking back to the house, Dick thought whimsically that a three-year absence had robbed him of some of his desert breeding. Nobody walked if there was a horse to ride. He remembered old man Naylor, whose house was on one side of the road and the mailbox on the other. Yet, rather than walk a few yards for his mail, old man Naylor used to saddle a horse and ride. Dick grinned to himself.

He entered his bedroom and from a bureau drawer took a dismantled .22 rifle. Dick assembled it, glanced through the bore to make sure it was unobstructed, and dug under some blankets for a box of cartridges. He prowled out into the cactus to look for his supper.

A jack rabbit bounded away and he brought the rifle to his shoulder. His first shot kicked up dust on one side of the fleeing rabbit, his second was short, and by the time he was ready for a third, the rabbit was out of range. But the next big-eared jack rabbit he saw, he stopped with the first shot. Dick skinned and dressed his game.

Carrying it back to the house, he brought two pails of water from the nearest water hole, started a fire of dead palo verde branches and the wood from a mighty saguaro that had toppled in the yard, put a pan of water over to boil, and laid the cut-up rabbit in it.

While the rabbit boiled, and it could use a lot of boiling, Dick cleaned his house and made up his bed. Finished, he tested his dinner with a fork, but failed to penetrate the tough meat even slightly. Finally he put the pieces of boiled jack rabbit on a plate, poured himself a glass of water, and sat down to eat. It was a slim meal, and a tough one, but it would do until morning.

At half-past five, wholly refreshed, he was up and ready to go. Sunrise in the desert was wonderful everywhere. He'd just never seen it in the city because there were too many buildings in the way. Dick brought Croppy in, saddled and bridled him, and mounted. He let Croppy buck it out, then started back down the road. Interested in what lay about him, Dick forgot that he had had no breakfast.

A whole forest of saguaro rose above the greasewood and Dick studied them as if he had never seen them before. Shallow-rooted, like most cactus, the saguaro presented an outward array of needle-pointed spines. Beneath was a smooth, tender skin that clung tightly to a framework of wood. The wood in turn supported an intricate inner layer of pulpy cells where, in time of rain, the saguaro stored water against those times when there was no moisture. A thirsty traveler, if he did not mind something that tasted remarkably like glue, could break a saguaro, suck the pulp, and survive until he reached a water hole.

The arms on the various saguaros twisted in every conceivable direction and grew at every imaginable angle. There was no conventional pattern, and Dick had heard that the Saguaro's arms occurred because the plant itself was shallow-rooted. A high wind might tilt it one way or the other, and when that happened it grew a compensating arm to balance itself. Some of the giant saguaro Dick looked at were older than the redwoods of California.

Trotting through the saguaro forest, Dick reached the road, turned Croppy down it, and at length reined him in in front of Blake's store.

A wooden building, the store had been built long before Dick's father was born and hadn't been painted

since the original coat was applied. At one time it was
supposed to have been under siege by Apaches. Still
imbedded in the front door was a metal arrowhead that
Enos Blake claimed had been left there in the battle.
Others said it had been driven in by Enos as an adver-
tising attraction. Posted beside it was a bulletin that
gave a full account of the fight and a notice indicating
that copies of the bulletin could be had inside. At one
time or another, probably during a minor earthquake,
the store had tilted on its foundation. There were those
who asserted that Blake had pushed it a bit more because he wanted people to guess when, if, and how it
would fall over. A hitching post that might have been
the original one and certainly looked the part, was out
front of the store, and over the door hung a bleached
steer skull.

Genuine or not, the store had a definite, appealing,
old-west atmosphere that Enos Blake was smart
enough to maintain. He did a thriving business because
tourists were attracted by the outside, and within, Enos
himself carried out the motif. A tall, spare man who
might have stepped out of the pages of any western
novel, he invariably dressed in cowboy boots, faded
levis, an equally faded shirt, and always on his head or
within easy reach was a ten-gallon hat. He came happily forward to meet Dick.

"Manuel told me you'd come back," Enos said, "an'
right glad I am to see you. Place hasn't been the same
'thout a Hartson round these parts. Had breakfast?"

"No," Dick admitted with a grimace. "I ate jack rabbit for supper and didn't want it again for breakfast."

Enos laughed. "Then I reckon you hit the right place.
Mother's just fixin' it. Come on."

He led the way into living quarters at the rear of the
store and Dick greeted Emily, Enos' pleasant wife. He
sniffed hungrily at the pancakes she was baking, the

sausage she was frying, and the tantalizing odor that escaped from the spout of the bubbling coffee pot. Expertly she scooped pancakes from the griddle onto two plates and laid sausage beside them.

"Now you two sit down," she told them. "Pancakes are good only when they're hot."

Dick ate, then ate some more. When he finally relaxed over his fourth cup of coffee, Enos looked questioningly at him.

"Back to stay?"

Dick nodded. "I guess my bed roll just naturally belongs here."

"Goin' to stay at the ranch?"

"Where else?"

"If you lack somethin' to do," said Enos, knowing very well that Dick had to have a job but not wanting to seem prying, "you might look for burros."

Enos pronounced it 'boo-roos.'

"Burros?"

"That's right. There was a fellow in here a few days back. Said people have took a shine to boo-roos, 'specially baby ones, for pets. Lookin' all over for 'em, this fellow was. He had nine an' said he can use a hundred more. He'll pay thirty-five dollars for every one he can get." Enos snorted. "Not too long ago you could've filled a box car with 'em and nobody would have paid two bits for the lot. But times have changed."

"I guess they have."

"They sure have," Enos asserted. "Last week some city folks stopped here to look at the ol' barrel cactus out front. Lady offered me ten dollars for it! Wanted it for a 'cactus garden,' Imagine that? People not only payin' ten dollars for a barrel cactus but even puttin' it in a garden?"

"Is that right?"

"That ain't the half of it," Enos continued. "Last year

I got offered five dollars for that steer skull on the hitchin' post. Somebody wanted to take it back to the city. Said he needed gen-u-wine western atmosphere."

"Did you sell?"

"Didn't sell that one, but I did sort of start gatherin' 'em up. City people pick 'em up fast's I can bring 'em in. No more'n three-four in the shed right now. They'll even pay money for rocks."

Dick's thoughts took a new trend. He could probably get a job if he wanted one. But he had come home to build up the C-2, and if he could do that without signing anyone's pay roll, he'd like it better. As Enos had pointed out, things seemed to be changing.

Formerly this desert country had been the home of a hardy few; people of hard work, vision, and courage. Struggling against tremendous odds, they had created an irrigation system and brought water to desert land. Now that land bloomed miraculously. Little by little the word had spread. Outsiders had come and were still coming. Manuel had told him that the city had mushroomed beyond anyone's wildest imaginings, and that land that Dick's father might have bought for a dollar an acre had been subdivided and sold for fifteen hundred or more a building lot. Many of the newcomers were well off, they liked the west, and they wanted to be western.

It would be years—Dick thought that he wouldn't see it in his lifetime—before the swelling tide of people overflowed the C-2. But their very presence might provide the wherewithal for him to acquire the desired flock of sheep.

Thanking the Blakes for his breakfast, Dick bought beans, coffee, canned goods and staples. He strapped his bundle on the indignant Croppy, then rode thoughtfully back to the C-2.

In the not too-distant past, and in a very real sense,

the entire Southwest had literally been carried on the backs of burros. The best and often the only means of transporting goods, whole trains of loaded burros had filed across the desert. Nobody who went into the desert could get along without them. Naturally some had strayed or been lost, and from these had descended large herds of wild burros. They had been hunted mercilessly; ranchers shot them because they ate forage that otherwise would have provided for cattle or sheep, numbers had been killed for dog food, and many more by those who simply wanted to shoot something. But there were still herds of wild burros in the country surrounding the C-2. Or weren't there?

To Croppy's great disgust, instead of being picketed at the water hole, he was mounted again after Dick left his groceries in the house. Dick knew every water hole in the area, and an examination of them would reveal whether many wild burros were using them. Dick rode out into the desert.

He halted on the slope of a hill that overlooked a water hole, tied Croppy to a palo verde, and with the .22 in his hands made his way to the rim of the hill. He didn't expect to see anything, for few desert dwellers moved about when the sun was hot. But there was always a chance of surprising something. He came to the top and stood quietly behind a big saguaro.

Presently he saw a coyote and kept intent eyes on it. There was a ten-dollar bounty on coyotes, but this one was hopelessly out of the .22's effective range. However, it might come nearer and he wanted to be ready.

What at first he thought was a wolf, but presently recognized as a greyhound, flashed into sight and hurled itself at the coyote. Dick stood spellbound, his eyes fixed on the fleet, tawny dog. Then it faded from sight in the greasewood.

What was a lone greyhound doing in the desert?

6. Trial By Fire

A third of the way up a rock hill, Tawny and Sable lay at the very rear of one of the natural caves with which the hill was pock-marked.

Still visible on the roof that arched over them was a layer of soot put there by the fires of ancient people who, long ago, had made of this cave a fortified home. The floor was littered with tumbled rocks and dirt that were all that remained of their fortification, and broken bits of pottery and a few spear and arrowheads were all that remained of their civilization. When these people lived here, the river below had flowed water to irrigate their corn, beans, pumpkins, and squash. The desert roundabout had been green. Now the river flowed sand and the desert was parched. Save for the vegetation around the water hole, the only present growth was cactus, greasewood, and palo verde trees which, some said, sent tap roots clear down to the water table.

Tawny and Sable had sought out the cave, not because it was cool, but because it was cooler than any other place they could find. The relentless heat of summer had descended. All day long a pitiless sun shone, and the heat was like a solid, invisible wall. It even penetrated into every crevice, crack, and cranny of the cave. But the heat was bearable inside, because there they were not in the sun's full glare. Close to the back of the wall, Tawny and Sable lay ten feet apart, chests heaving and tongues dangling as they sought what comfort they could.

In their own ways, other desert dwellers adjusted themselves.

Range cattle lay quietly or stood motionless, and when they did move, it was for only a few feet. Javelina panted in their daytime lairs. Jack rabbits moved very little, and even sand lizards and gophers were not active. Only the wild burros, that never seemed to care whether it was hot or cold or whether it rained or didn't, followed anything remotely resembling a usual routine. Save for a couple of scattered sprinklings, so meager that they did little more than lay the dust, there had been no rain for five months. Rainfall for the season was dangerously below normal.

A few feet from Tawny a great horned toad sat motionless until a red ant started up the cave's wall. The horned toad hopped over, paused a second, flicked its tongue out, and swallowed the ant. Then it stood as motionless as it had before. Partaking of the color of its surroundings, like all horned toads, this one had taken its hue from the cave's floor and dark shadows. It was so well camouflaged that Sable did not even see it. Tawny saw it, but watched indifferently. Knowing it for a harmless thing despite its ferocious appearance, he left the little lizard alone. It was too hot for even the smallest exertion.

Sable got up, panted slowly to the edge of the cave, and looked inquiringly at the water hole in the valley below them. He looked back at Tawny, who manifested no interest. Highly adaptable, the greyhound had taught himself to use water sparingly. Thirst bothered Sable more than it did him.

Sable did not go down to the water hole by himself. By nature he was a follower, so much so that he had made himself dependent on Tawny for almost his very thoughts. He went without question wherever his companion took him and did willingly whatever Tawny indicated must be done. Now he came back to the rear of the cave and lay down, his fur fluffed about him and his bushy tail extended straight behind. Paradoxically, Sable suffered less than Tawny from the heat. His heavy fur served as insulation while Tawny's short hairs did not.

As the sun went down, midsummer's humidity seemed to make the wall of heat more oppressive and more evident. There was no pleasant tang such as might be felt after a hot day in a northern climate. But, no longer exposed to the sun's full glare, the desert did cool slightly. Tawny prepared to leave the cave.

He got up, stretched lazily, yawned, and walked to the edge of the cave. A molten ball of fire in the west, the sun tinted the rocky hills with every shade of blue and purple. Roused from its daytime lethargy, a mockingbird perched on top of a spined saguaro and flooded the evening with song. Tawny eyed the mockingbird, saw a jack rabbit prowling about, and noted a herd of wild burros just coming in to the water hole.

Sable whined anxiously and nudged Tawny's shoulder with his pointed nose. They had entered the cave an hour after sunrise, been there ever since, and the puppyish Sable yearned to stretch inactive muscles. He frolicked ahead as they made their way down to the water hole.

Water dripping from their muzzles, the solemn burros raised their heads to stare. There were nine jennies with six foals, all jealously shepherded by a tough little roan jack. He stamped and made ready to repel the two dogs, who eyed him cautiously. They had never

bothered the wild burros because Tawny was not interested in them. But he had no intention of being driven
from the water hole.

The jack snorted angrily and rushed. Unwilling to
face such an apparition, Sable turned tail and ran.
Tawny stood his ground, and when the jack reached
him he slipped aside. Agile as a deer, the jack turned to
pound at him with flailing hoofs. But Tawny was no
longer there. He dodged again and rippled in to slash
the jack's flank. Whirling, the wild burro ran back to his
harem.

He stood his ground until all had drunk their fill.
Then, lingering in the rear lest the two dogs attack, he
herded the jennies and foals away. They crashed
through a thicket of staghorn cactus that might well
have stopped anything except a burro, and disappeared.

Tawny and Sable went in to drink. Without understanding what it was, Tawny realized that something
was happening to the water hole. It had been a pool
about twenty feet long by eight wide, with another,
smaller pool fed by the overflow. Now the small pool
was wholly dry and the sun had baked its bed to a
cement-like hardness. The other pool had shrunk to a
third of its former size, and had become an oval of still
water. The subterranean spring that fed it was failing
fast, and because it had so little fresh water seeping in,
the pool was both warm and brackish. But it satisfied
thirst, and after Tawny and Sable drank they set out to
hunt.

A coyote flashed before them and Tawny gave chase.
He gained on the fleeing creature, but was still a dozen
yards from it when the coyote slipped into a dry wash
and turned along its sandy wall. Losing sight of his
game, Tawny abandoned the chase.

It never occurred to him that this was the first coyote

he had seen in two weeks. Some of them, like the wise pack of wild dogs, had gone into the cooler peaks for the summer. Many of those that would have spent a normal summer on the desert had followed when the water holes started drying up. Born to the desert, they knew it as Tawny and Sable did not and were aware of what was coming.

Tawny returned to Sable, who greeted him with wriggling enthusiasm. All the affection that normally would have been lavished on a master, Sable had transferred to Tawny. The greyhound was the pup's hero, and the smallest thing he did was right. In turn, Sable gave Tawny the companionship he needed.

They passed a gaunt range cow that braced her feet and stared at them. After they passed, the cow resumed nibbling at the slender branches of a palo verde. Like most desert plants, the palo verdes were thorned, but the hard-mouthed range cattle were used to them.

Tawny paid no attention when he flushed a jack rabbit that normally he would have chased and caught. Oppressive heat did not inspire great hunger, and Tawny wanted to choose his game. He was looking for javelina, and a half-hour after seeing the jack rabbit, they came upon a herd.

The wild pigs were trooping slowly down a trail, stopping now and again to eat, as they worked slowly toward the water hole. Bristling, their young behind them, they faced the two dogs. But Tawny had learned how to handle javelina and Sable, having been slashed by one, had achieved a healthy respect for them.

Sable yapping hysterically beside him, Tawny rushed the herd. He had discovered for himself that some javelina are more nervous than others, and one or two usually broke and ran when they were rushed. Those could be pulled down, but Tawny wanted one of the young.

Sure that nothing could hurt him as long as he was near Tawny, Sable stayed at his companion's shoulder. He, too, knew this technique, and was prepared to turn when Tawny drew up short and whirled. Two barren sows broke and ran, giving Tawny the moment he needed. He leaped among the scattered animals to get a piglet and was away before there could be a return rush. Unexpectedly, confused by the dogs' attack, the herd raced away in sudden panic.

Tawny and Sable went in to their feast. They ate as much as they wanted and for an hour afterward busied themselves cracking bones to get at the sweet marrow within. Finally Tawny stood up and licked his chops. When they started out again, they chose a leisurely pace.

By nature both restless and a long ranger, and possessing a large bump of curiosity, Tawny's habits differed radically from those that another dog in the same situation might have established. Finding food, water, and an area that suited his tastes, another dog might have been satisfied in a comparatively limited range. But Tawny liked to roam, and Sable stayed with him, perfectly willing to go wherever Tawny went. Together they not only covered a large portion of the desert, but were intimately acquainted with everything in it.

Presently Tawny halted at sight of a white-faced desert cow and calf.

He knew all the cattle in his range and the water holes where they drank, and usually paid little attention to any of them. He was attracted to this cow and calf because he had never seen them before and wanted to know why the calf was acting in such a strange way.

Standing near a giant saguaro, the calf braced itself on widespread legs. Its head drooped weakly, as though it had no strength left, and its muzzle all but brushed the

ground. The anxious cow nuzzled her offspring until
the calf took two trembling forward steps. It stopped
again, unable to go on, and as Tawny and Sable
watched, it collapsed like a slowly deflating balloon.
Head bent to her calf, the cow tried to make it get up by
shoving with her muzzle.

Tawny and Sable did not know it, but these two had
already had their trial by fire. Ranging a part of the
desert which Tawny had not yet visited, the water hole
upon which they'd depended had finally seeped out to
a mud puddle and then gone dry. The pair had set out in
a search for water and the calf was already done, with its
mother not much better off. Domestic animals, they
were the first to die of thirst, for comparatively few
range cattle learned how to get water from cactus.

An hour later, when Tawny and Sable returned that
way, the cow was gone and long-eared little kit foxes
were quarreling over the carcass of the calf. Both dogs
rushed, and the foxes scattered like shadows before
them.

With daylight, Tawny set his course for another water
hole near which he intended to lie up during the day.
He led Sable down for their morning drink, but halted
in dismay.

Two days before, the last time they'd visited this
water hole, there had still been a little water. Now there
was only moist mud whose crust was hardening
rapidly. Pushing his nose into it, Tawny succeeded
only in filling his mouth with mud. He cleansed his
tongue by scraping it between his teeth, and opened
and closed his jaws. Mouth gaping, mud-flecked
tongue lolling, he raised his head to look about him.

Thirty yards away, a flock of quail were flitting about
a clump of cholla, sipping from the trunks the few drops
of dew that had formed there during the night. Desert-

born and bred, the quail knew how to help themselves when surface water disappeared. Tawny and Sable could only suffer.

Sable scraped hopefully and energetically with both front paws. He sniffed at the hole he made and looked enquiringly at Tawny. Instinct had driven Sable to do the right thing, and had he dug deeply enough he would have found water. But both dogs had too many years of domestication behind them to know that.

Tawny turned away and Sable padded woefully behind him. They faced a serious problem and knew only one way to solve it. Since there was no water here, they must go to another water hole. They climbed a ridge, and in the far distance Tawny saw buzzards wheeling in the sky. The cow they'd met last night had left her calf and gone as far as she could. Now, with the eternal patience of their kind, the buzzards were waiting for her to die.

The sun blazed higher into the sky. Reflecting from the desert floor, it turned it into a seething furnace. Tawny slowed to a walk and Sable lagged ten paces behind him. Younger than Tawny, and not as adjusted to the desert, he was feeling thirst more acutely. But they must go on; there was nothing else they could do.

Tawny raised his head suddenly and his ears pricked up with as much interest as he could muster.

A hundred yards away a wild sheep, a slat-ribbed old ewe, stood beside a tall saguaro. Paying no attention whatever to the long, needle-tipped thorns, she dipped her head, bit deeply into the saguaro, and complacently chewed the pulp. The old ewe took another bite, and another. Then, warned by a wild thing's keen senses, she looked around, saw Tawny and Sable, and clattered hastily off. Tawny paused beside the saguaro and sniffed at the spot the ewe had bitten out.

He was too tender-mouthed to bite into such a thing,

but the old ewe had already torn the thorns away. Tawny licked the oozing wound, then took a mouthful of pulp. Surging eagerly forward, not even whimpering when he struck his nose on a thorn, Sable stood beside him. They swallowed water-laden cactus pulp until even their slender muzzles could reach no deeper into the wounded saguaro, and for a while they rested beside it.

Tawny went on, partly because his good sense told him that it was better to do so, and partly because the sun's direct rays were torture to his short-haired skin. The saguaro's pulp had eased his thirst enough so that he could trot again, and revived Sable sufficiently to enable him to keep pace.

Past mid-morning, they came to the water hole they had been seeking. Formerly a sizable pool, it had shrunk to a shallow basin. But they could drink, and both dogs lapped until they could hold no more. Panting, they flung themselves down in the shade of a cottonwood.

Their roots deep in the ground, the five big cottonwoods and the single date palm around this water hole still remained green. But at its edges, the carpet of green grass had shriveled and turned brown. By nightfall, scarcely a dipperful of surface water remained. There was enough to furnish a drink apiece, then Tawny caught the first jack rabbit that flushed before him. He was becoming nervous.

He had stayed in the desert by choice, because of his great need for freedom. His own intelligence and adaptability had fitted him to get along there, so far, but nothing had prepared him for this. Vivid in memory was the exhausting, heat-blasted trek of the morning. He had no wish for another such experience, and now that he had found water, he feared to get very far from it.

At daylight Tawny and Sable came in for their morn-

ing's drink to find the water hole in possession of a wild
burro so old that the hair on his head and flanks had
long since turned grey. Born on the desert, the wisdom
of age added to inborn cunning, he had not seen anything for years that could frighten him.

When Tawny and Sable approached, he merely
glanced at them and resumed scraping mud with a hard
hoof. Fresh mud lay on all sides, and so vigorously had
the old burro scraped that there were mud flecks ten
feet behind him. Already he had a hole fifteen inches
deep, but it was not deep enough. The old burro continued to scrape until the hole was adequate. His job
finished, he dozed on his feet. Fifteen minutes later he
awakened, drank the water that had seeped into the
hole, and went his unhurried way.

Bracing their paws in the bottom of the hole, Tawny
and Sable took the old burro's place and drank the
water as it seeped in. They were eager but the water
came slowly, so that it was fifteen minutes before they
had enough. Again they lay up in the cottonwood's
shade.

That night Tawny and Sable sniffed at the nowdry
water hole. Again Sable scraped hopefully and again
failed to dig deeply enough. Neither dog could get
more than a few sips of water and what they drank was
laden with mud. Tawny set purposefully off through
the desert.

He had known what to do before when they found a
dry water hole and he knew what to do now. Eight
miles away, in a direct line, there was more water. But
Tawny's course between the two had never been a
direct one. Dog-like, he had deviated for whatever took
his fancy. Now he took the course he knew best.

When a jack rabbit skipped before him, he ignored it.
Thirst was too demanding to give even a slight thought

to hunger. Both dogs' tongues lolled, and in the dark night their short breaths were very audible.

Tawny led Sable into a dry wash. Sand-floored most of the time, the washes flowed water in times of rain and might even be flooded during a heavy downpour. Even though the floods were years apart, they were sufficiently strong to sweep shallow-rooted, slow-growing desert plants out of the washes. Most traveling animals used them as highways because there were few obstructions. Range cattle, mule deer, wild burros, bobcats, coyotes, and even jack rabbits used these washes.

Tawny climbed out of the wash and broke into a trot that became a run. The water hole was only a short distance farther on, and he and Sable could drink. Tawny raced past the cottonwoods that grew near the water hole and stopped in his tracks.

A dead cow, neck outstretched and tongue extended, lay on the baked hardpan where the water had been. A kit fox slunk away, but there was no other sign of life. The water hole had been dry for a week and not even a wild burro had been scraping at it.

The panting Sable touched Tawny hopefully with his nose. Tawny expressed his own terrible thirst in a little whine and went on. He must have water and the next water hole he knew was the one near the sheltered cave. It was a fearfully long way, but Tawny knew of no other water.

Another scorching day bloomed redly. Tawny did not even look around when a lazy jack rabbit hopped out of the way. Jack rabbits seemed able to exist with or without water. Deer, herds of which existed for years without any surface water known to humans, crunched cholla, and the wild sheep bit into saguaro. Sooner or later, if no rain fell, all the desert animals would be in

trouble and many would die. But the animals that had
learned to live with man, and to look to man to supply
their needs, were already in trouble.

Grunting its misery, a blocky range bull with its head
hanging so low that its nose almost brushed the ground,
passed in front of Tawny and Sable and bumped
squarely into a big saguaro. Unseeing and uncaring,
almost dead from thirst, the bull continued to work its
legs as though it were some huge mechanical toy that
had been wound up and could not run down. Uncaring,
the dogs went on.

Lagging behind Tawny, Sable's head was hanging.
His tongue lolled full length, but very little moisture
dripped from it for Sable had little left. Rising like a
mirage in the distance, the rocky hill that fed the water
hole they were seeking shimmered in the enveloping
heat. But it was too far away.

Tawny descended into a dry wash. He was walking
very slowly, scarcely more than plodding, and spells of
dizziness assailed him. When Sable cried out, he
turned. The collie had fallen, and was trying to get up.
He struggled to a sitting position , braced himself with
both front feet, rose, and came on unsteadily.

As though it had sprung from the desert itself, there
was a coyote before Tawny. For a moment he stood still,
puzzled because he had not seen the animal come from
either side of the wash. The coyote leaped into the
cactus and disappeared. Too thirsty and too nearly done
to give chase, Tawny plodded on. A few steps beyond
the place from which he had first seen the coyote, he
snapped his head erect and pricked his ears up. He
smelled water! Tawny broke into a near-crazy run, and
came to the hole from which the coyote had emerged.

At varying distances beneath the surface of the
washes were beds of rock, and some such beds form
catch basins that hold surface seepage. Coyotes, trot-

ting along the washes, smell that water and dig down to it, sometimes as much as ten feet.

This coyote had had to dig only four feet, and Tawny squeezed into the hole frantically. Life-giving water wet his parched tongue and mouth. He lapped as though he could never get enough and was only vaguely aware of the frantic Sable trying to crowd in beside him. Tawny withdrew and Sable drank.

Just before nightfall, they reached the water hole in the rocks. It was low, but still contained water. Many things drank there now. There were wild burros, deer, antelope, bobcats, javelina, foxes, all the thirst-tortured creatures that had not been able to find water on the desert. When Tawny and Sable arrived, a bobcat was drinking almost within reach of a desert cottontail. Both had endured the fiery desert hell to get here. Neither had a thought for anything save water. When Tawny and Sable came up to drink, the rabbit hopped a few feet and sat quietly. The bobcat, licking his dripping chops, paid no attention.

That night, a setting sun turned to purest gold the blue-shadowed peaks of the Lost Angels. Tawny stared fixedly at them, then turned his gaze on the desert they had left. He looked again at the mountains.

The peaks were still sun-lit when Tawny and Sable started their climb into the mountains.

7. High Country

High on the pine-shaded side of Two-Face Mountain,
Dick Hartson reined Croppy to a halt and turned in the
saddle to look for Molasses, his pack burro. Two minutes later, the laden burro came in sight. The pack he
carried seemed almost bigger than he was. But it was
not as heavy as it looked, for a fair share of it was Dick's
bed roll and the rest consisted of enough groceries and
camp equipment to keep him in the Lost Angels until
he felt like coming down. Neither increasing nor de-
creasing his pace, Molasses came to a halt behind
Croppy and switched his tail.

Dick had found Molasses a month ago. Riding
Croppy in comparatively open desert, he had almost
decided to circle a patch of mistletoe-laden mesquite
when impulse made him ride through it instead. Hoping to escape detection, Molasses was hiding in the
center of the thicket and flushed only when Dick came
through. Immediately Dick gave chase.

In spite of the fact that burros are slower than horses,
for a while the outcome of the chase had been in doubt.
Molasses could twist and dodge with all the agility of a
ground squirrel trying to escape a coyote, and Dick

missed the first two casts with his rope. On the third try, his loop settled neatly around Molasses' neck.

A wild horse or cow would have fought the rope, and at the very least would have choked itself before finally submitting. Molasses was too smart. His was the calm philosophy of a burro, and he had no intention of hurting himself. He let Dick lead him back to the C-2, where kindness plus judicious bribes of dried prunes, a delicacy new to Molasses, did the rest.

Breaking him to pack had presented some difficulties, but not too many. Molasses' ancestors had carried the burdens of humanity almost since there had been any mankind, and he soon accepted the inevitable. His one fault was his speed, or rather, lack of it. Except for those very rare occasions when he saw reason to hurry, Molasses had one slow pace.

Ducking his head, he now started eating thistles. Dick glanced down at Molasses' pack, saw that nothing had worked loose, and turned to look at the desert below.

It stretched as far as he could see, and from this height the more distant desert hills looked like mere knobs. The air was so clear that he could see individual cacti and trees, and here and there a patch of still-bright green that marked a water hole. Dick leaned forward to rest his elbow on the saddle horn and he cupped his chin in his hand.

He hadn't done too well since he'd come home, but neither had he done too badly. Besides Molasses, he'd caught five baby burros, and found a ready market for them, as Enos Blake had said. A sign along the road, 'Cactus For Sale,' hadn't attracted any individual buyers but it had brought a nursery owner who specialized in cactus gardens. He had wanted saguaro, of which not one in twenty was fit for the cactus gardens city people wanted. Dick had found some small but good specimens for him, and had been paid a nominal fee for them.

Dick had had one windfall. The Trail Man's Club, a group of hardy souls devoted to outdoor adventure, decided to serve rattlesnake meat at their annual banquet. Most of the Trail Men found it much pleasanter to talk about hunting rattlesnakes than to get out and hunt them, and they'd offered Dick fifty cents each for all he could bring in within a stated time. In two days, Dick had gathered a hundred and twenty-six.

In addition he'd found and sold some turquoise and netted twenty dollars from a collector for a near-perfect chunk of translucent pink quartz. Off days he'd worked for Manuel Gomez or shot a few coyotes and bobcats for the bounty.

Though he probably would have earned more money had he taken a steady job, he liked it better this way. If there was uncertainty, there was also the possibility of a lucky streak. Maybe he'd even be able to start his flock of sheep this fall, although he had no illusions about starting in a big way. If he was able to buy as many as ten good ewes and a first-class ram, next spring's increase should double his flock and he could build from there.

Now he had come into the high country partly to hunt wild burros and partly to escape the desert heat. As he looked over the endless miles, he thought of the desert creatures and of what they were enduring in this year of little rain. Usually there was water here and there throughout the area, but this summer the only water holes he knew of that still flowed were those on the C-2.

He started Croppy and rode on up the slope, the philosophical Molasses plodding behind. They hadn't gone far before Croppy flicked his ears forward, arched his neck, and snorted softly. Prancing a little, he pretended to be spooky. Dick took a firmer grip on the reins and looked around to see what Croppy had smelled.

To one side, about fifteen feet from the course they were following, was an abandoned ant hill. At one time it had been a big colony; a circle ten feet in diameter was almost bare of grass where countless thousands of burrowing ants had left a sandy waste. Scattered about the sand were the remains of a deer.

Dick halted Croppy, dismounted, rein-haltered his horse, and went forward. It could not be a lion kill, for lions did not scatter their kills around in such a fashion. It looked like wolf work, but as far as Dick knew there were no wolves in the Lost Angels. He decided that it must be a lion kill which coyotes had found and dragged about. He picked up a splintered thigh bone that had been cracked by powerful teeth, and frowned. Maybe a coyote could splinter a big bone in such a fashion, but he doubted it. Dick got down on his hands and knees to look for tracks in the ant hill. He found what he thought were wolf tracks; certainly they were too large for coyotes.

As far as was known, there were no wolves in the Lost Angels, but maybe not everything was known. It was a big country, and throughout the year not more than a dozen men came into it. A pack of lobos might conceivably have worked down from the north or up from the Mexican border. If so, it was bad. A pack of wolves killed an enormous amount of game.

Dick's eyes strayed to a blackberry cane on the far side of the ant hill. He walked over, picked up the bit of hair that clung to the cane, and looked at it closely. Beyond any doubt, the hair had come from a dog. Judging by its texture, color, and tight curl, Dick guessed that it was some kind of terrier, probably an Airedale. Since dogs and wolves do not hunt together, it followed that the tracks had been left by dogs.

Dick got down to study the tracks again. They varied in size considerably, and he judged there were four or five different sets. Obviously a pack of dogs had killed the deer. Could the greyhound he had seen been one of them?

Dick thought of the .22, the only firearm he had. He knew that some of the unwanted dogs cast loose in the desert managed to survive. Several such survivors must have banded together; the very fact that they were here in this high country and had been able to kill an adult deer was itself evidence of an organized pack. No casual stragglers could even catch a deer, unless it were injured. Besides, stragglers would hardly be this far up in the mountains.

Although there had been no rain, the tracks had a weathered look and sand had fallen into them. The wild pack, Dick decided, had been here about a week or ten days ago.

Molasses, having caught up again, was dozing behind Croppy. When Dick started toward them, the burro opened his eyes, twitched his long ears, and trotted to meet him. Grinning, Dick took a dried prune from his pocket and held it out in the palm of his hand. Molasses licked it off, crunched it happily, and looked hopefully for another.

"You wait," Dick chided. "If you had your way, I wouldn't do anything except feed you prunes."

He mounted Croppy and rode thoughtfully on. Most outlaw dogs became such because some human being was at fault, either by abandoning them or by being cruel enough so that they ran away. Some, given the right master, could not only be redeemed but were smarter dogs for having run wild. But they were not many, and a dog that had run wild was always an uncertain quantity. The best course was to shoot them; a band of wild dogs killed as much game as a pack of lobo wolves. However shooting them was easier thought about than done because, when they acquired the ways of wolves, a wild pack also learned the wariness of wild creatures. In fact, they could be far more dangerous than wolves, having once lived with humans. They knew the ways of people and how to circumvent them, and they seldom hesitated to extract such tribute as they wished. Dick was glad that he hadn't any sheep this season. A flock would not be safe in the Lost Angels as long as a wild pack roved there.

While thinking these things, Dick gained the top of Two Face. He looked about with pleasure.

He had come to a vast, forested plateau. Twenty miles to the north, a still higher peak thrust farther into the sky. The belt of timber, like the circle of hair on a partially bald man, ended a thousand feet below the craggy heap of rocks that formed the summit. Patches of snow still clung to the sheltered sides of the rocks. It was Lost Man Peak, and there were various stories as to how it had come by its name. All of them centered about some lost man, for there had been many since the first buck-skinned trappers had pushed into this country.

Dick felt the rising exaltation he always experienced whenever he came onto this plateau. It was lonely, but he liked lonely places. A sense of complete freedom and of well-being enveloped him. Whatever money he had lost by not taking a steady job was well sacrificed if he could come into the Lost Angels whenever he felt like it. He put Croppy to a trot.

An hour after reaching the summit, he came to a broad meadow that was thatched with short green grass. A dozen mule deer, grazing in the meadow, raised their heads, looked at him for a moment, stamped their feet, and moved toward the forest. They stopped a few yards short of it, turned to look again, and resumed browsing when nothing threatened.

There were not many water holes even in this high country, and one of the best of them was in this meadow. A great spring formed a round pool forty feet in diameter, and the overflow became a narrow streamlet that flowed across the meadow and through the forest, leaped down the slope, and ten miles farther on became part of a bigger creek. Fed by snow water, the spring was always icy cold, and there were trout in the stream. Not many people fished in this inaccessible spot and Dick was sure the trout would be plentiful.

Dick stripped Croppy's bridle and saddle, looped a thirty-foot picket rope around his neck, and tied him to a tree, for Croppy had a bad habit of heading for the ranch when opportunity presented. Taking the hatchet from his saddlebags, Dick cut a picket pin, led Croppy down to the creek, drove the picket pin into the ground, and tied Croppy to it, within easy reach of grass and water.

Twenty minutes later, Molasses ambled into camp and stood waiting to be unloaded. Dick removed the pack, stripped Molasses' sawbuck-shaped packsaddle, and picketed him near Croppy. Molasses would never run away as long as he carried a pack because he was smart enough to know that he could not rid himself of the load without help. But he might get ideas if he hadn't any pack.

Then Dick set about making camp. A shelter was not necessary because there was little more likelihood of rain in the high country at this season than there was in the desert. Even if it did rain, Dick's sleeping bag was waterproof. But he needed a fireplace.

He cut two crotched sticks, drove them into the ground so that the crotches were even with each other, and laid a green pole across them. His coffee-pot and kettle he hung on wires from the pole. Bringing rocks from the meadow, he built a fireplace and hunted until he found a flat rock big enough to lay across the top. Then he hung his food packs and sleeping bag on the down-sweeping branches of a big pine. Camp was complete.

From his pocket Dick took a coil of line and a plastic leader box containing snelled hooks. He tied a hook to the line, slipped the flat box back into his pocket, and while Croppy watched curiously and Molasses dozed, he overturned rocks in the meadow and pounced on the fat black crickets he found beneath them. He dropped the crickets into the cut-off foot of a woman's nylon stocking, brought along for the purpose. The crickets' serrated feet caught in the nylon webbing and they couldn't climb out.

Dick went to the stream, cut a willow pole, tied his line to it, baited with a cricket, and cast into a dark riffle. At once a trout surged up to the bait. Dick struck and missed, but he caught the next trout. Missing two more, he caught four in succession. They were rainbow trout and not large; the biggest Dick had was about nine inches long. But they were good eating, and had been fished so little that there was a strike at almost every cast.

While working his way downstream, Dick passed a whole thicket of ripened and ripening blackberries. Finally getting his sixth trout, Dick cleaned his catch and wrapped the trout in wet moss that he took from a little side eddy. He stopped on the way back upstream to pick a hatful of blackberries, then returned to camp.

Filling his coffeepot and kettle with water, he started a fire, and slid both receptacles over to boil. When the kettle was boiling, he stirred a handful of rice into it and just before the rice was cooked added another handful of raisins. With a stick he shoved the coffeepot and kettle away from the fire and fried his trout.

Crisp trout, boiled rice and raisins, and fresh blackberries, made more than a satisfying meal when washed down with black coffee. Dick stamped the fire out and was about to wash his dishes in the stream when he glanced across the meadow. The mule deer were gone, but three cow elk that had come out to feed were staring at him. Evidently he wouldn't lack for visitors.

With darkness, Dick spread his sleeping bag in the meadow and crept contentedly into it, grateful for its warmth. The desert was scorching, but even in summer, nights in this high country were not only cool but cold. A billion stars, so close that it almost seemed he could knock them down with the fishing pole, bloomed overhead. A distant coyote chorus lulled him to sleep.

In bed with darkness, he was up with dawn. He'd come to hunt burros, and seeking them in this high country would be different from hunting them on the desert. There it had been necessary only to make the rounds of the water holes, find which ones were being used by wild burros, and plan accordingly. In the high country, with the whole creek at their disposal, the burros would not have to confine themselves to water holes.

However, he had discovered that wild burros were creatures of habit. Left unmolested, they used the same paths, grazed in the same places, and usually drank from the same pools. Dick breakfasted, saddled Croppy, and while the still-picketed Molasses watched indifferently, started slowly down the stream.

He found where deer drank and saw them leaping away as he approached. They were not unduly alarmed, for last hunting season was long past and the next one still to come. Bouncing on legs that seemed made of rubber, they stopped to look over their shoulders before finally running on and disappearing in the forest. Then a herd of cow elk, calves skipping at their heels, faded away in front of him, followed by a big lone bull, velvet-covered antlers laid back over his shoulders. Dick found where a lion had been drinking, then, three-quarters of a mile from camp, finally located what he was looking for.

The meadow ended there and tall trees pressed closely on both sides of the little creek. Just within the trees a distinct path trailed out of the forest, and on it were imprinted the oval, unmistakable, hoof prints of wild burros. Dick leaned from his saddle to study the tracks. There were at least six of the burros, he decided, and though he could see no foal tracks among the many left by adult animals, there was a good chance that a herd this big would have young with it. In the creek was still a faint trace of roily water, so the burros had quenched their thirst very recently, probably at dawn.

Dick marked the place in his mind and rode on down the creek. He found where a single burro had been drinking and he did not stop. The lone beast was doubtless a surly old outcast from somewhere, and he didn't want adults. They were harder to catch, harder to manage, and didn't sell nearly as readily as the foals.

Two miles from the first drinking place, Dick found where a larger herd of burros had been coming to water. There were at least twenty, and obviously had been bothered very little. They hadn't made even a slight attempt to hide their sign, and the path they used was as well beaten as a pasture trail. There were sure to be young with such a herd.

Dick rode back to camp, satisfied.

The next morning he was up an hour before daylight. He tested the wind to determine its direction, saddled and bridled Croppy, but did not mount. Instead, he led his horse to the lower end of the meadow and into the forest. He halted where he could see the place from which the smaller herd of burros had been drinking, but at the same time remain unseen. Wild burros were wary as deer and a lot smarter. They would not knowingly walk into a trap.

In the thin light of very early dawn, he saw them coming. There were four jennies, two with babies beside them, a red jack, and a younger jack. Heads bobbing, they filed down the path and lined up to drink. Dick waited until they'd had their fill, then in one motion swung into the saddle and urged Croppy forward.

Wasting no time to identify what was coming, the little herd wheeled and clattered away. Dick gave Croppy his head and the little bay responded. He'd done this before and knew what to do now. Keeping his eyes on the running burros, almost as agile as they were and faster, he drew up on the fleeing herd. Dick shook his rope.

The baby burros were as fast as their elders. But they lacked endurance for a long run and already were lagging behind, their mothers dropping back with them. Dick threw his loop, snared the first baby, and Croppy stopped in his tracks. While its mother raced on, the baby burro ran to the end of the rope and tripped.

Dick swung down from the saddle. A pigging string, a shorter length of rope, in his hand, he seized the struggling foal, tied its left front to its right rear leg, left it lying on the ground, and coiling his rope as he ran, he mounted Croppy again. The other foal was tired too and now was the time to get it.

He drew near, swung his loop again, and caught the second baby burro. The rest of the herd ran on. Dick dismounted and gathered up his captive.

It was an appealing little mite, all long legs, flopping

ears, big eyes, with the whole held together by a wisp of a body. No wonder they were in demand as pets, Dick thought; they were even more winsome than a puppy. He stroked the baby gently.

"I know," he soothed. "It's mean to take you from your ma. But you're going to a good place, little guy. There won't be any coyotes or cougars to chew you up, and all you'll have to do is sleep, eat, and maybe carry some youngster on your back. Bet you'll like it."

The foal turned trusting eyes on him. Though some of the adult burros fought captivity, even most of those submitted without too much fuss. The babies, too young to have learned that it's a hard world, tamed almost at once.

Dick led the little creature behind him and stopped to get his first captive. Returning to camp, he staked them near the somnolent Molasses, picketed Croppy, and went fishing again. Two baby burros were worth seventy dollars. It was a good day's work.

At dawn the next morning, Dick was hiding in the forest near the place from which the big herd had been drinking. The sky lightened fast and the sun came up, and they did not appear. Dick knew then that he had made a mistake. Wild burros were very wise. Probably, on his previous visit, he'd left some sign that they had detected and now they were watering elsewhere. Dick rode down the creek to find the big herd's new watering place.

An hour later he realized that they were no longer drinking from the creek, which meant that they had forsaken it for a water hole. But they wouldn't leave the country; and the very fact that they had been drinking from the creek was evidence that their favorite pasture was not too far away. Dick thought of the nearest water hole.

It was a small pond situated near a slope. The overflow, trickling down the slope, left a trail of mud behind it, then lost itself in a crevice. There should be tracks, at least. Dick mounted Croppy and rode through the forest. Nearing the water hole, he dismounted and led the bay. If the burros were here, he did not want to alarm them a second time.

He stopped in startled surprise to see a dog, a young tri-colored collie, scoot away from the water hole and disappear in the forest. Dick reached for his rifle, but did not shoot. Little more than a puppy, this dog was scarcely one of the savage, polished hunters that had pulled down the deer. What was such a young dog doing here? Dick was within fifteen feet of the water hole before he saw the collie's companion.

Only its head protruded from the mud in which it had buried itself. Its eyes were closed, but it was not dead for its breath came in short, choppy gasps. It opened its eyes when Dick came nearer. Too weak to run, it did not try. The dog was a greyhound, and though there might be two greyhounds loose in the Lost Angels, Dick doubted it. This must be the one that he had seen run down the coyote.

But what was the matter with it?

8. Running Fight

Tawny's ascent into the Lost Angels had been uneventful. The devoted Sable following faithfully, he had struck the straightest course he could into the high country. Though they'd gone without water all night long, shortly after dawn they'd followed a doe and fawn into a little grove of pin oaks and found a water hole there.

This was different from the desert they'd left behind. Though there was still cactus, for the most part it consisted of prickly pear and cholla, and that scattered here and there; there were no cactus thickets. The saguaro did not grow this far up, and though there was an occasional barrel cactus or staghorn, they were few and stunted. This section of the Lost Angels had mostly pin oaks, chaparral, mesquite, and scattered bunches of dwarf cedar.

After drinking, Sable went off exploring on his own and practically stumbled across a jack rabbit that did not see him in time. Hysterical with joy and swelling with pride over this, the first jack rabbit he'd ever caught, Sable worried his kill and played with it before he finally lay down to eat. Tawny caught a rabbit of his own; then, for the balance of that day rested in the pin oaks. The sun was not quite as fierce as on the desert, but they hadn't yet climbed high enough to reach cool country.

That night they traveled on again and before dawn were on the plateau. There both dogs reveled in the first cool breeze they'd felt for six weeks; it was so refreshing that they did not lie up when the sun rose, but explored the woods. Neither had ever been in such a forest, and if they were somewhat nervous because they did not know exactly what to do, they were also interested in what it had to offer.

Chance alone brought them to the water hole. Roaming through the forest, they trotted out into a little meadow, came upon the muddy overflow, and followed it back to the pond. The water was cool and tangy, wholly unlike the tepid, brackish stuff they had been drinking on the desert, and after they slaked their thirst, they went for a swim. Only the tops of their heads and their noses protruding, they swam about for five minutes. The cold bath gave them energy that neither had felt on the desert and made them really hungry for the first time in weeks.

Climbing out of the water, they shook themselves vigorously, then Tawny led the way into the pine forest. The trees were more than a little puzzling, for until now he had done all of his hunting in comparatively treeless country. But, as usual, he was confident of his ability to take care of himself no matter where he happened to be.

A quarter-mile from the hole, they found one of the wild pack's old kills, another deer that had been dragged down about two weeks before. Sable busied himself snuffling about. Tawny, who used his nose only infrequently, did not. The deer would have interested him only if there had been anything left he wanted to eat.

Tawny trotted on, head erect and turning constantly

so that he would miss nothing. Depending on his eyes, he had to see his quarry before he could run it.

He caught a flicker of motion at one side and stopped to stare fixedly in that direction. Clearly he saw a small, silver-grey creature scraping busily in the pine needles. Never having seen such an animal, Tawny did not know what it was or how it might act. However, he was pretty sure that it would be good to eat, and he rushed forward.

The long-eared squirrel had only to scamper four feet to a pine, spring into it, and climb the first limb. There, as though bored with the whole proceeding, the squirrel scratched its right ear with its right hind foot and flicked its tail derisively.

Baffled, Tawny watched speculatively, and stored the whole incident away in his brain. Obviously, just as this country differed from the desert, so did some of the creatures inhabiting it. He'd have to change his methods of hunting; the next time he saw a long-eared squirrel he must get nearer before he tried to run it down.

His confidence unshaken, sure that he would find something he could catch, Tawny led Sable on. Twenty minutes later he was again attracted by a bit of motion and stopped in his tracks. The first lesson had penetrated and he did not need a second. Very slowly, Tawny started soft-footing toward the source of the motion. Sable, who hadn't seen anything, followed cautiously. Tawny stopped behind a big pine and peered around its trunk.

Three wild turkeys, young gobblers, were feeding on grasshoppers in a little open glade. Although they lacked the ripe wisdom of older birds, they were still alert. All three never fed at the same time, but while two caught grasshoppers, the third stood sentinel with head erect.

Unseen and unmoving, Tawny studied them intently. He knew what they were doing, but not what they were, and he wanted to make no mistake this time. Luck was on his side. Unaware that they were being watched, the three slowly fed toward Tawny. One raced to catch a grasshopper and the greyhound made his rush.

The three saw him instantly and whirled away. Heavy-bodied, they needed a little run before they could be air-borne. They labored into flight and would have escaped from a slower dog than Tawny.

Leaping six feet into the air, he set his teeth in the thigh of one of the gobblers and bore it to the ground. Powerful wings hammered him and the gobbler's free claw raked his head and face. Tawny closed his eyes and hung on. Sable, rushing in, clamped his teeth on the gobbler's neck and the meal was theirs.

As the days went on, Tawny's old restlessness returned full force. While on the desert, he had not confined himself to any one water hole, and he did not limit himself here. Leading Sable cross-country, he found the stream where the wild burros watered. Swinging in a great arc intended to bring them back to the first water hole, they discovered another. As the two dogs traveled, they learned.

There were elk, deer, and wild burros in this high country, but Tawny had never hunted the bigger game on the desert and he did not do so here. When a shuffling black bear raced in panic before him, he chased it only far enough to nip its heels a few times, then abandoned the chase. But Tawny discovered that much of the small game he'd found in the desert also inhabited the plateau.

Spotted throughout the forest were broad parks, or meadows, and they were favorite eating and playing places of both jack rabbits and cottontails. In addition, there was a different kind of hare, the splay-footed snowshoes that wore a brown coat in summer and a white one in winter. There were also gophers and ground squirrels, chickarees, and long-eared squirrels. Foxes prowled this high country, and Tawny caught and killed two coyotes. He found mottled bobcats and slinking lions, wild turkeys and dusky grouse, and even javelinas.

Indirectly, one of these latter brought disaster.

Within five hundred feet of the first water hole they had found, Tawny and Sable pulled down a javelina and ate part of it. Then they drank, rested, and when they were hungry again started back to get what was left of the javelina. They walked carelessly, paying little attention to what was about. Since their next meal awaited, there was no reason to be stealthy.

Danger came about so suddenly that Tawny was unaware of it until too late. A four-foot timber rattler, lying in wait beside the path the two dogs chose, uncoiled his spring-steel body and sank venom-injecting fangs deep into Tawny's right shoulder. There was not even a warning rattle.

Tawny recoiled, instantaneously aware of intense pain, but filled with a hot surge of sheer anger. He flung himself on the snake and was struck again. Before there could be a third strike, he killed the snake. In a spasm of wrath, he tore it to shreds.

Wide-eyed and uncomprehending, Sable only stared. Tawny stood on shaky feet, pain spreading throughout his body. The trees and shrubs that he had seen so clearly shimmered and danced in front of his eyes. He lowered his head to sniff at the fragments of snake that lay about, and grew dizzy.

Tawny's mouth was hot and dry, so that instead of food he wanted water. The frightened Sable tagging questioningly at his heels and his head drooping, the greyhound made his way back to the water hole and drank. Then he waded in. It was no applied intelligence that made him do so; Tawny did not understand the nature of, or the treatment for rattlesnake venom. He only knew that cold water eased the burning fever that was beginning to beset him.

Sick, he was not as yet too weak to understand what was going on. When his head dipped beneath the surface and his nostrils filled, he swam weakly out of the pool and crawled into cool mud at its outlet. Tawny stumbled and the mud seeped about him. Struggling, he dragged himself closer to the edge where the mud was more shallow.

He was only half conscious when Dick Hartson found him, but with Dick's coming, a wonderful dream enfolded him. It was not Dick at all, but the beloved Fred Haver, who had really come. Tawny welcomed him in a happy daze, and when he felt Dick's soothing hand on his head and nose, it seemed to be Fred's hand.

All that day and all night he lay still, too feverish to know or care what was taking place much of the time, but rational enough at intervals to know that Sable was lying beside the pool. Having gone only far enough to eat from the dead javelina, too frightened and bewildered to leave Tawny, the young collie could only wait.

The next morning, though he was still very sick, Tawny's fever had lessened and he could move a little. He heard Croppy approach, and when Dick came down to the water hole, Tawny felt that he should run. But he was still too weak, and he did not really want to. Yesterday's dream was still with him, and though he knew now that his visitor was a stranger, it seemed to Tawny that he had seen him before. Dick Hartson was not Fred Haver, but he was almost like Fred, with his gentle hands and understanding voice.

"Poor old fellow," Dick soothed. "Poor sick dog. I brought you something."

He held out a dish of warm broth. Tawny sniffed at it and turned away. He had no appetite, but when Dick left the dish of broth and rode away, the eager Sable came out of the brush where he had been hiding and lapped it all up.

While cold mud eased his diminishing fever, Tawny slept the morning away. He felt better when he awakened, and when he heard Croppy again he looked anxiously up. He'd been hoping for another visit, and did not flinch when Dick patted his head.

"You're better," Dick murmured. "You're better, dog, and it looks as though you'll make it. Maybe you can eat a bit now. Bet your pal got the other."

He poured warm broth from his canteen into the dish he'd left that morning and held the dish where Tawny could reach it. Tawny lapped a few mouthfuls, rested, then drank half the broth. He wanted no more, and Dick put the dish aside.

"You're going to make it, dog, and some dog you are! I'll just let you rest until morning, then come back and get you. If you come along I think your pal will too, and I can use both of you. You'd be right handy dogs to have around a ranch."

Dick rode away and Tawny watched him go. He wished almost desperately that Dick would stay, and as he disappeared, Tawny whined. He continued to watch the game trail up which Dick had ridden Croppy until the tail-wagging Sable came out of hiding and stood before him. Now that his mentor was regaining an interest in life, Sable's cup of joy was running over.

When the long shadows of evening slanted over the water hole, Tawny dragged himself from the mud. He stood on shaky legs, and nipped when Sable would have frolicked with him. But now that Tawny had started to win back his health, his recovery was fast. He had conquered the venom, and needed only to regain his wasted strength.

Had Dick been there, Tawny would gladly have gone with him. But convinced that Tawny could not possibly recover for several days, and not wishing to upset or frighten him while he was sick, Dick had stayed in camp.

Tawny turned toward the place where the javelina lay. He bristled when he passed the dead rattlesnake and continued on to the dead wild pig. Sable had done a thorough job there; not much except polished bones remained. While the collie watched, Tawny chewed one.

They went back to water, then traveled into the forest, and lay up in a snarl of little pines. They were still there when Dick came back to the water hole the next morning, found both dogs gone, and returned to camp, bitterly disappointed.

In the little pines, Tawny's sleep was restful rather than feverish, and when he finally awakened he was hungry. He prowled the forest with Sable, and when a jack rabbit flushed in front of him, he gave chase. But he was still weak, and his speed failed him. He went back to the thicket and slept again.

While the hungry Sable prowled to see if he could find food for himself, Tawny remained in the thicket. A long-eared squirrel came scooting through, alert for whatever moved but with no eyes for what did not. He all but overran the resting dog, and Tawny had to do little more than snap his jaws to catch the squirrel.

He ate eagerly, and was feeling much stronger when Sable came sadly back. In search for food, he'd found and bounced at several rabbits. But he hadn't caught any, and it was both frustrating and mystifying because he'd seen Tawny run rabbits down. However, his own failures served to make an even greater hero of his companion. Sable found a patch of blackberries which, while not filling, had been something to eat. He sniffed around and gobbled up the few bits of squirrel that Tawny had not eaten.

They went back to the water hole, drank, and Tawny rested again. Then he hunted and caught a jack rabbit. After sleeping a short time, he caught another, which he shared with the grateful Sable.

With full recovery came great hunger. Rests grew shorter and hunting expeditions more frequent. Tawny couldn't get enough to satisfy the demands of his restored body, let alone providing for Sable. The next day, with the collie pacing behind him, Tawny set off toward a park where rabbits abounded.

They entered the meadow and trotted through it side by side. Tawny kept his head high the better to see, and his eyes roved constantly. His technique was to walk with Sable until they flushed a rabbit, and then run it down. There was little point in running fast before there was anything to chase. However, though there always had been numerous rabbits here, now there were none.

They were halfway across the park when the reason for the scarcity of rabbits appeared. Tawny glanced to one side and saw the wild pack sweeping out of the forest on the far side of the meadow.

Brutus led, the rest stringing out in their order of speed. Tawny's anger flamed and a growl bubbled in his throat. He recognized his old enemies of the desert and knew that he and Sable could not fight all five. Tawny began to run.

He did not flee because he wanted to, but because he must. Anger flared in his heart and the fierce eyes of a fighting-mad greyhound burned in his head. He slowed his pace deliberately, half-minded to stop and fight anyway. If one or more of the wild pack got too far ahead of the others, Tawny would happily offer battle.

He heard a mingled yelp-snarl from Sable and whirled around.

Instead of running at once, the puppyish Sable had stopped to stare inquisitively. Then, discovering that Tawny was running, he had finally awakened to the fact that the wild pack was hostile. It was too late.

Brutus had overtaken him near a big grey boulder that arched out of the meadow. Rowdy and Bull were closing in to help, while Pal and Joey, in the rear, were yelping encouragement.

Tawny wheeled and raced back, anger flaring.

Sable cried again, but now he voiced more than terror and a puppy's appeal for help. Sable's ancestors were collies that seldom fought for the sake of fighting alone. But they never lacked courage; never showed a coward's streak. Sable turned to engage his enemies.

Tawny saw Brutus dive in to lunge low and seize Sable's shoulder. The collie slashed back, but he knew little about fighting. Brutus threw him end for end, and Sable collided soddenly with the boulder. For a split second, stunned, he lay still. Then he rolled feebly and tried to get up. But his legs were no longer strong enough to hold him.

The greyhound voiced his battle cry. About to swarm over Sable, the wild pack turned to face Tawny. Like the smooth-running unit they were, they combined forces to kill him. Then, at their leisure, they could finish Sable. Brutus took his position two yards in front of the feebly moving collie. The panting Rowdy flanked his right shoulder; Pal and Bull took their stands, at his left. Joey, too small to be of much use in battle, circled about the others.

The wild pack had fought before, and its hard-bitten

members were past masters at it. But Tawny, too, had lived in the wild, where harsh existence had sharpened his naturally keen brain. Enraged, he was not ruled by blind hatred, but surveyed the field as he ran, to determine his best strategy.

Tawny and the wild pack were a breath apart, when, from the edge of the forest, came the snap of a .22 rifle. As though he'd suddenly decided to stop all his frenzy, the circling Joey quieted and wilted to the ground. Instantly the rest of the pack broke and ran. The rifle snapped again and again.

Too enraged to have a thought that did not concern his enemies, Tawny did not realize that Dick Hartson, riding nearby when Sable first yelped, had galloped Croppy to the scene. Coming within range, he had sighted on Brutus as the leader. But he'd reined Croppy to an abrupt halt after a hard run, and Croppy plunged twice. Missing its intended target, Dick's bullet had caught Joey in the head and dropped him in his tracks. By the time he was ready to shoot again, the wild dogs were four racing, dodging targets.

Knowing only that at last his enemies were in flight and that their usual formation was broken, Tawny raced at Pal, who was nearest. He drew alongside the fleeing renegade and measured his pace to the pointer's. This was a technique he'd learned on running coyotes and he used it to good advantage now. Setting his teeth in Pal's neck, Tawny stopped suddenly. The abruptly halted pointer smashed his nose into the ground and flung his hind-quarters into the air. Tawny was upon him before he could get up. His powerful teeth sought the spine, just behind the place where head and neck joined. Pal went limp.

With no second thought for him, Tawny raised his head to look for the others. He leaped high the better to see, and sighted Brutus within twenty feet of the sheltering pines. The greyhound launched himself at the wild pack's leader.

However, though the fight with Pal was over in seconds, those seconds were enough to give Brutus a start. Tawny was thirty yards short of the trees when Brutus disappeared within them.

A hound would have set its nose to the ground and trailed, but Tawny did not know how to trail. Losing sight of Brutus, he lost him entirely. But his blood was up and his alert brain realized that the wild pack was scattered. Now was the time to find and fight them.

Tawny paused with his front paws on a fallen tree and looked all around. When he saw something move, he flew instantly at it. But it was only a peaceful old buck that, resting in a favorite bed, had made the mistake of twitching an ear and had thus betrayed himself. The buck sprang up and ran. Paying no further attention once he'd identified the deer, Tawny let him go, and continued searching for the wild pack.

Not until after nightfall did he concede failure. Once in the forest, the remaining members of the wild pack had been completely swallowed by it. His tongue lolling, very tired, Tawny drank from the stream and set his course for the park where the fight had begun.

The two dead members of the wild pack lay where they'd fallen, but there was no sign of Sable. Tawny whined and paced restlessly back and forth. He had always had great need of speed, freedom to use it, and love. Deprived of any one of these three, he was desolate.

Tawny sat down, pointed his slim muzzle at the sky, and wailed his heartbreak to the cold, uncaring stars.

9. Sable's Conquest

Even as Dick Hartson continued to shoot at the wild pack, he was aware of the futility of it. Not only were the dogs running very fast, but the .22 lacked the smashing power of a heavier rifle. When the rifle's bolt finally clicked on an empty chamber, he lowered the weapon to watch Tawny's fight with Pal.

As he watched, his admiration gave way to crushing disappointment. He knew now that, instead of waiting for Tawny to get well, he should have taken him while he lay in the mud. Since Tawny had been in no condition to run or fight back, his capture would have been relatively easy. But that opportunity was gone forever and so probably, was Tawny. The wilderness into which he fitted so well had claimed him again.

For a long time Dick stared at the place where Tawny had disappeared, then brought his gaze back to the meadow.

He'd arrived just as Brutus threw Sable, and Brutus' command of the pack was so obvious that Dick had known him at once for the leader. The rest might break up if the strongest and smartest dog, the one to which the others looked, could be disposed of. Dick had done his best and had succeeded only in killing Joey. Dick felt a pang of regret because he had done so, but at the same time knew that before long somebody would have to shoot or poison the rest. Wild dogs, roaming in a pack, were as bad as wolves—worse, because they were less afraid of humans.

Dick reloaded his rifle, feeling a rising anger toward the thoughtless or careless people whose misuse of dogs was responsible for packs such as this. He looked hopefully at the woods where Tawny had disappeared, and wished the wonderful greyhound luck. Well, he was gone and better forgotten.

But Dick couldn't forget him. Try as he would to banish it, Tawny's image kept appearing in his mind—a very symbol of that desert freedom that meant so much to Dick himself. Such a dog deserved a better fate than the one he would meet. Apparently the wild pack had been ranging this country for quite a while, although its presence was evidently not yet known. But eventually they would betray themselves, and when they did, a game warden, ranger, or trapper would be sent in to get them, and the greyhound would be hunted down, too. The wild dogs were destined to be caught in traps or to die from bullets or poison, and no trapper or hunter, while he was at it, would spare Tawny.

Dick had a sudden inspiration. Enos Blake had been a trapper and must still own traps. He would loan some to Dick. Maybe, if the steel jaws were well-padded, he himself could catch Tawny without hurting him. If so, he could at least try to tame him. Dick pursed his lips thoughtfully and considered what he should do.

So far, he hadn't located the big herd of wild burros and had succeeded in catching only the two foals he had at camp. He wanted more, and it would make no difference if he stayed a few extra days. Tawny would still be here.

Dick was about to turn away when he heard a dog

whine. The sound was so unexpected that he whirled, rifle ready in his hands. At once he lowered the weapon.

Seized by Brutus, Sable had suffered little except a torn shoulder where the big dog's fangs had gripped him. Thrown, he had collided with the boulder so forcefully that the effect had been like a heavy blow on the head. Lapsing into unconsciousness after his first few feeble attempts to get up, Sable had come to again and struggled to a sitting position. Bracing himself partly against the boulder and partly on stiff front feet, he was blinking his eyes, a dazed expression on his face.

Dick had forgotten about the collie, but now looked at him thoughtfully. Nobody could be sure that any wild dog was redeemable. The older ones were sure to be set in their ways. But this one was still very much a puppy and might be brought back to man. Dick moved slowly toward him, and made reassuring sounds when Sable flattened his ears and lowered his head.

A growl rumbled in the collie's chest and he looked suspiciously at Dick. Sable, who had been tossed willy-nilly into a life that never would have been of his own choosing, really wanted only to love and be loved. He shrank close to the boulder as Dick came nearer, and turned his head away. Vaguely he wished Tawny were here because his mentor would know what to do. But the young collie only shivered and closed his eyes.

The hands that touched his matted coat were gentle and the voice that fell on his receptive ears was gratefully soothing.

"Poor little pup," Dick murmured. "Don't be afraid. Just because some nitwit that didn't know a good dog when he had one tossed you out to live or die, you don't have to be afraid of me. I won't hurt you."

Sable opened his eyes and turned his head. Still unsure of himself, not daring to believe this was a friend, he kept his ears flattened. He sniffed tentatively at Dick's hand, and in spite of himself the tip of his tail began to jerk tremulously back and forth. A sense of warmth and well-being came over him. He quivered but did not cry out when Dick touched his wounded shoulder and aching head.

"You're not hurt bad, pup. That big grey devil ripped your shoulder and you bumped your head when he threw you against the rock. I think that's all."

Sable heaved a mournful sigh and blew through his nose. Had he been older, and of a different nature, he would already have adapted himself to a wild life. But Sable was a born man's dog, and in addition, one of the many creatures that will never lead but must always follow. Sable sensed in Dick the same strength he had found in Tawny.

He sighed again and laid his head on Dick's shoulder when Dick gathered him up. He made not the slightest protest when Dick laid him across Croppy's saddle bow and mounted behind him. If this human thought such a procedure was right, then right it had to be.

Dick walked Croppy back to camp. The bored Molasses did not even look up, but the two baby burros flicked long ears and danced excitedly. Very young, they had tamed so readily that Dick had allowed them the freedom of the camp one day after their capture. It was necessary to tie them only at night or when he was away.

Dick dismounted and lifted Sable down. His headache passing, the collie pup was again on his feet. His plumed tail wagged continuously, his brown eyes shone, and his jaws framed a happy canine smile. Dick watched for a moment. But far from dashing away the second he was free, Sable would venture no more than six inches from Dick's heels.

The collie turned his head to watch gravely while

Dick dusted his wound with sulfa powder from a first-aid kit, then tagged along when Dick went down to loose the baby burros. The long-eared foals switched wispy tails and readily accepted this latest addition to their circle of acquaintances. Never hurt, the baby burros hadn't the faintest conception of an enemy and knew no reason to fear anything.

The collie pup and the baby burros sniffed each other thoroughly, but Sable left his new-found playmates and followed closely when Dick led Croppy to water. Having found a master, Sable was taking no chances on losing him.

That evening Sable feasted royally on beans, bread, and half a can of corned beef hash. Nothing else was needed to win the collie's heart completely. While the night deepened and the leaping fire glowed progressively brighter, Sable lay with his head on his paws. As close to Dick as he could wriggle, he shivered with delight when Dick petted and talked to him.

"I was going to get me a dog," Dick told him. "Now I've got one and it's sure better this way." He stared into the darkness. "Wish I had your pal, too. You're all right. But he sure is some dog!"

Out in the forest a young deer, separated from its companions, bawled mournfully. Sable raised his head to look and pricked up his ears. Dick continued to stroke him gently. It seemed that, right here, he had most of the things he'd ever wanted: a horse, a dog, a comfortable camp, and freedom to do work he liked. He wouldn't ask another thing.

That is, he wouldn't if he'd never seen that greyhound.

Dick grinned ruefully. Sable, as he had known the first time he saw him, was a good dog. In time, with training and experience, he would be a valuable one. If he lacked courage, he never would have stood against the wild pack. But his necessity for depending on some being stronger than himself had already made itself evident. Sable would willingly do whatever he thought Dick wanted done and most dogs were like him.

The greyhound stood apart, and Dick kept trying to define the elusive quality that made him so. Vividly he remembered the wild, free way Tawny had caught the coyote, and his running fight with Pal. Even when the sorely stricken greyhound lay in the mud, there had been something that marked him as different from ordinary dogs. Dick saw in him the same quality that Fred Haver and John Weston had seen, but to Dick it was all good.

He sighed wistfully. Then he set his jaw and planned.

He had food for three days more if he didn't stretch it, and perhaps five if he did. He'd hunt the big herd of burros for at least three days, unless he found them sooner, and see if he could catch some more foals. Then he'd go back to the desert, renew his supplies, and return with traps. Maybe he couldn't tame Tawny even if he caught him. But he'd certainly try.

Dick nodded sleepily, yawned, and sought his sleeping bag. When Sable tried to crawl in too, Dick pushed him away.

"Hey! There's room for only one in here!"

Sable lay down so close that his furred back brushed the sleeping bag. Dick petted him, smiling. When this young collie adopted a master, there were no halfway measures.

In the thin, cold dawn, when Dick awakened, Sable sprang up and danced eagerly around him. The collie pups' eyes were bright and sparkling, mischief-filled, and his jaws framed a constant grin. Obviously he had fully recovered; even the wound on his shoulder was healing.

Dick crawled out of the sleeping bag, hastily donned a jacket, picked up a stick of firewood, and threw it. Entering wholeheartedly into the spirit of the game, Sable galloped after the wood, snatched it up, and brought it back. Dick interrupted his fire-building to rise and throw the stick a second time. Almost at once, the stick of wood between his jaws, Sable was back and pleading with him to throw again.

"Go away!" Dick ordered firmly. "If I play with you all morning we'll never get started."

The wood clutched in his jaws, Sable hovered hopefully near. When Dick did not offer to play with him, he dropped the wood, raced full speed to another stick and brought it. Willing to do anything to oblige, and with no end of sticks available, Sable intended to give Dick a full choice.

As the collie brought the sticks, Dick broke them across his knee and added them to his fire. Puzzled, but still eager, Sable continued to offer sticks that Dick might throw for him. Dick rubbed his ears.

"You're right handy," he said with a grin. "Wait'll I tell Manuel and Enos that I've got me a dog that collects firewood!"

Sable padded courteously beside him when Dick went to bring Croppy, raced ahead to renew his acquaintance with the baby burros, then ran full speed back to camp. His youthful spirits surged like a cataract and his body was just not big enough to contain his new-found happiness.

When Dick mounted Croppy he came and wagged an anticipatory tail. Then, looking bewildered, he sat down and flattened his ears. Momentarily puzzled himself, suddenly Dick understood and laughed. Yesterday Sable had ridden, and he wanted to ride again.

"Come on, walk!" he said. "You were an invalid yesterday, but you're not today!"

Finally understanding and gracefully accepting this turn of events, Sable paced happily beside Croppy when Dick started out. Dick forgot him and concentrated on the problem at hand.

He'd found evidence of the big herd of burros only once, the first time he'd ridden down the creek. Thinking the burros set in their ways, he had been careless. So doing, he had not only alarmed his quarry, but apparently he had frightened them right out of existence. Though he'd been in the saddle all day and every day since, and had twice seen the herd from which he'd taken his two captives, the larger herd had vanished. They were no longer drinking from the creek, Dick knew, because he had ridden almost to its mouth, nor were they visiting any of the known water holes. He had been unable to find where they were grazing, either.

That was a minor point, for a burro or goat would grow fat where any other grass-eating animal might starve. But the herd had to be watering somewhere. Dick did not believe they'd gone down into the desert, though they might if hunted hard enough. However, this herd had not been hunted at all. They knew only that there was a human around, and that should not stampede burros.

Dick thought they had a secret water hole, one he did not know. Nor did it seem likely that he was going to find it.

For an hour Sable trotted faithfully beside Croppy, and when he strayed at all he never ventured more than a few feet away. Growing more venturesome, he lingered to sniff about a thicket, then galloped furiously to catch up.

Warm, but not unpleasantly hot, the sun rose to its noon peak and Dick shed his jacket. Finding it a bit warm for frolicking, Sable walked behind Croppy, and when they neared a water hole he knew, he waited hopefully until he was sure Dick intended to visit the place. Then he ran ahead to enjoy a drink and a cooling swim.

For the remainder of the day, Dick searched the plateau. It was a frustrating and somewhat aimless hunt, for he had already examined all the places where he thought the herd might be and knew definitely that they were using none of the water holes with which he was familiar. He was still certain that the burros had not left the plateau and was just as sure that they were drinking somewhere. When and if he found their watering place, he would find the herd.

That night, having failed again, he returned to camp. With next morning's dawn he started out to resume the hunt. Sable tagging amiably alongside, he rode back to where he had first found evidence of the herd. There he walked Croppy slowly up the trail, leaning from the saddle and studying sign as he did so. Deer and elk had used the path recently, but no burros had left their oval hoof marks on it. He reined in and stared toward Two-Face Mountain.

The sky-reaching peak seemed to be within easy walking distance, but this air was so clear that judging distance adequately was very difficult. The base of Two-Face was actually nineteen miles away, and the nearest water Dick knew was within three miles of its lower reaches. Burros could go that far to water, but Dick did not think this herd had done so. He clung to the opinion that, somewhere, they'd found a different drinking place that he did not know about.

The country between the park and the mountain was the only area he hadn't searched, and he'd kept out because he knew of no water there. Naturally, giving it a complete inspection would take him weeks rather than days. But Dick could go through a small part of it and cover the rest in successive trips from the plateau. Besides the possibility of finding the herd, it would be a distinct advantage to discover a hitherto-unknown water hole. Such a place might well be used as a base for future operations.

Sable, who had discovered for himself that Croppy usually trotted or walked, had found also that he could catch up with the horse whenever he chose. This gave him a chance to explore the million fascinating sights, scents, and sounds on both sides of the trail. But he never ventured so far that he couldn't return to Dick in a minute or two.

The rising sun warmed the uplands and stole much of Sable's youthful exuberance. Panting heavily, he came in to match his pace to Croppy's. Dick dismounted, drank from his canteen, poured water into his hat, and let Sable drink. The collie pup lapped thirstily and looked for more, but Dick screwed the cap back onto his canteen.

"Not now," he said firmly. "You'll have to wait awhile. There may not be any more water until we get back to camp."

Croppy, desert-bred, would need no drink until tonight. The strong little horse stood switching his tail, and started willingly when Dick remounted. They crossed a park, rode into forest on the other side, and Sable streaked past Croppy to run into a thick tangle of young evergreens.

Dick grinned as he watched him go. Besides being good company, Sable's antics provided a never-ending source of amusement. Probably he didn't even know where he was going now or what he intended to do when he got there, but he wouldn't be out of sight for very long. Croppy trotted and Dick continued to look for burro sign.

Presently Sable careened back out of the little trees

and waited. Seeing him, Dick reined Croppy in abruptly.

Sable's soaking wet fur clung so tightly to his body that he seemed half his former size. Even his ears dripped water, and water dribbled down his chin as he charged happily up.

Dick dismounted, reached down to pat Sable's head, and peered into the little trees.

They hid the answer. He hadn't found the water hole he was seeking because he had assumed that there would be an outlet or overflow. Instead, this hidden water hole must pour its surplus into some subterranean outlet.

Leading Croppy, Dick started slowly into the little evergreens.

He could not have explained how he knew the missing burros were drinking here. It was a hunter's instinct, a sixth sense dominant in primitive man but so little used by modern man that few still possess it. Often, without seeing anything, Dick had been aware of the presence of a deer, elk, or antelope. Now the same feeling told him that he was not only near the burros' drinking place, but within easy reach of the burros themselves.

Dick slowed to a cautious walk. This herd was wary and he had already spooked it once. He didn't want to do it again. Through an opening in the little trees, he caught a glimpse of the water hole. It was a small pond ringed by a narrow belt of green grass which in turn was hemmed in by trees. Evidently a spring fed it and some fissure drained the surplus as fast as the spring flowed, so that the water level varied little. Dick saw the burros and stopped. They were just approaching the water hole from the far side.

With a hysterical yelp, Sable left Dick and streaked around the pond. Dick turned to Croppy so quickly that he startled the horse into a nervous plunge. Trying to quiet him and mount, Dick swore in annoyance. Evidently the burros hadn't seen Sable before, but now, with the pup hot after them, they were bouncing into the forest.

Dick gave Croppy his head and rode around the rim of the water hole to overtake the burros. Frightened by the barking pup, who probably thought he must protect Dick, the herd was already out of sight. There was little hope of catching any, but Sable's hysterical yelling still sounded in the forest. Trying to dodge face-whipping branches, Dick rode directly toward the sound.

Dodging among the trees, he overtook the running burros, Sable doing his best to make them run faster. Dick set his loops and made for a foal that had fallen behind. He swung, made his catch, tied it, and remounted. Sable's frenzied barking continued to waken echoes.

Dick caught a second baby and was off again. Sudden silence reigned as Sable stopped barking, and Dick came upon him in a little glade. He was licking the face of a third foal that had fallen behind. Dick dismounted and scooped the baby up in his arms. Eyes big with pride, Sable reared to sniff his new friend.

"I don't know," Dick gasped, "why I ever bothered with you! But I'm sure glad I did!"

That night, back at camp, Dick and Sable lolled before the fire. Dick was contented. The day's search had turned out far better than he'd dared hope; five young burros were worth a hundred and sixty-five dollars. Now he must take them down, renew his supplies and borrow Enos' traps, and come back up. A vision of Tawny arose to tease Dick, then weariness overcame him. He stretched, yawned, and was about to pull off his boots when Sable sprang erect and growled.

Dick tensed, peering into the black night. He put out

his hand to touch the pup and felt him bristle. There was no sound and he could see nothing. But obviously Sable had a scent that he did not like.

The deep silence was broken abruptly by Croppy's scream of fear. The horse neighed again, and there was the sound of running hoofs, then an audible snap as his picket rope broke. Croppy galloped off into the night.

Dick snatched the rifle with one hand, the axe with the other. Sable snarling beside him, he ran toward the baby burros.

10. Killer's Stalk

When Brutus leveled out to catch Sable, he hadn't the least doubt as to the outcome. Three years in the wilderness had taught him the measure of his own strength and speed, and to catch and kill this fleeing puppy would be a simple matter.

He was a little surprised when Sable turned to fight, for not only dogs but most other creatures preferred to keep on running when the wild pack was on their trail. Still, killing Sable would be no more than a momentary interruption, and Brutus' main attention centered on Tawny, whose reactions were always unpredictable.

He remembered the greyhound with special hatred, for Tawny remained the one creature that had not only defied, but had dared fight the wild pack. To catch and kill him now would be a special triumph. But Brutus had little real hope of it, for vivid in his mind was Tawny's incredible speed. Even though they'd hunted hard, the pack had not been able to get him before. But they could at least kill off his companion.

Brutus overtook Sable almost exactly where he had expected to, easily dodged the pup's snapping jaws, and using both his own strength and Sable's speed, threw him end for end. Turning for the routine task of killing the young collie, he saw Tawny coming back and instantly prepared to meet him. Sable could be dealt with later. Then Dick Hartson's .22 snapped, and Joey crumpled.

Brutus reacted instantly, but not blindly. He did not know exactly what had happened, but he did know that he was in unexpected danger, and ran instinctively.

Even as he fled, Brutus' anger flared. For three years the pack had ruled everything it found, and his leadership had brought a great arrogance. Thinking himself invincible, it angered him to have to run away, as lesser creatures had fled from the pack.

As soon as he was within the forest, he stopped and looked around. He saw Dick Hartson and Croppy, and Tawny coming very fast. Brutus glided to one side and stood quietly behind a tree while the greyhound raced past. He did not challenge Tawny because he knew the greyhound was at least his equal, and he would never voluntarily match his own strength against an enemy that might defeat him. Besides, the man was still there.

As Tawny flashed past and disappeared, Brutus discovered the other's weakness. He had slunk behind the tree to hide from the man, and he fully expected Tawny to find him there. Any of the pack members would have smelled him, but the greyhound did not.

Brutus let him go. Tawny had been marked for death by the pack, and in time the pack would kill him. At the moment, it was more important to escape the man and to find Bull and Rowdy.

A brisk breeze blew from the park to him, and carried with it the strong scents of Dick Hartson and Croppy. Sure of himself because he was in forest where he knew he couldn't be seen and Dick was still in the park, Brutus slunk to the edge of the trees and peered out. He saw Dick gathering Sable in his arms, and hatred flared in the Alsatian's eyes. But caution ruled him. Much as he'd like revenge on Dick, the only being that had ever routed the wild pack, to go back into the meadow now was too dangerous. Brutus slipped away, and when he was deep enough in the forest, he trotted along, looking for his companions.

Presently he met Bull and Rowdy, besides himself all that was left of the wild pack, in a little open glade that had served as a pack rendezvous. They stood shoulder to shoulder, hostile and suspicious as they awaited his coming. Brutus, their leader, who was responsible for keeping the pack out of danger, had failed.

As he neared the pair, Brutus sensed their rebellion and knew that he must quell it at once. He met the situation with customary craft.

Trotting, as though he intended merely to join the pair, he did not attack until he was very near. Then, whirling, he laid Bull's shoulder open and twisted around to slice Rowdy's neck. Rowdy yelped his pain, and the yelp had its effect on Bull. About to try conclusions with Brutus, he drew back. The leader faced them, snarling.

The other two cringed. For three years Brutus' brains had not only held the pack together but had guided it to good fortune. His craft was complemented by that other requisite of all tyrants; sheer physical force. Brutus was stronger and could fight better than any other dog in the pack, and all knew it. Thus, even though Rowdy and Bull no longer trusted him, they feared him too much to do anything about it.

Almost contemptuous of his followers, Brutus struck into the forest, the rebellious pair following. Brutus suddenly stopped when he caught the scent of a deer.

Hungry, the pack had been hot on the trail of another deer when Brutus had seen Tawny and Sable and diverted the pack to them. Now they must hunt again, and it was his place to find game. Brutus slunk toward the deer he had scented. He was still thirty yards from it when the deer smelled him, snorted sharply, and leaped away. As Brutus bounded toward it, the deer went out of sight and hearing.

Brutus ran as fast as he could toward the place where he had last seen the deer. But all he saw now were grey-black trunks and green branches of the coniferous forest. Brutus made a great, methodical circle. He returned to the last place he had seen the deer, dipped his muzzle to the ground, and snuffled deeply of the hot scent that clung there. He raised his head uncertainly and looked all around, baffled.

Dick Hartson, shooting Joey rather than Brutus, had shot better than he ever knew. Brutus had supplied the brains of the efficient pack, and along with Rowdy, Bull, and Pal, made up the fighting force. But Joey had provided another indispensable ingredient; a keen nose and an inborn ability to follow tracks. Pal could be replaced, but losing Joey was like losing the key gear of a machine.

Again Brutus sniffed the deer's scent. Once more baffled, he raised his head to look. Trailing game was no part of his nature and necessity had never forced him to learn. It would now, but time must pass before Brutus mastered the art of finding game by following tracks. The remainder of the pack was in for some lean times.

Rowdy and Bull hung back, glaring suspiciously at their leader and waiting for him to do something. It had never occurred to either of them to wonder why they had usually fared so well. They were part of the pack, and each knew his place and duties to perfection. But they were followers, and since joining the pack, neither one had even tried to find his own food. They merely helped pull down what Joey trailed and Brutus out-maneuvered, and earned their share because they were able to help with the final kill.

Brutus traveled on, and the hunger in his belly mingled with the anger in his brain to form a searing acid that inflamed his fury. The wild pack had been supreme until the man came along. Now its rule was threatened and Brutus knew it. Twice more he raced at deer and saw them run away from him. Aware of their leader's seething fury, Rowdy and Bull maintained a respectful distance. Catching no other food, they visited an old kill and crunched up and swallowed the meager bits that remained.

Hunger set them prowling after a short rest, and in the misty dawn of the following morning Brutus snapped up a cottontail that flushed almost beneath his nose. Holding the kill between his paws, warding Rowdy and Bull off with snarls, he ate all of the rabbit. They coursed throughout the day, and when Rowdy caught a chipmunk he swallowed hastily, even while Bull and Brutus lunged to take it away. Again failing to find food in adequate amounts, they visited other old kills and tried to stay their hunger with crumbs. The once-proud wild pack, that had never been satisfied with anything except fresh, hot kills, was scavenging for carrion.

The three had become disorganized, irritable, and perpetually suspicious of each other. Unless they fed soon, and well, a finish fight among the three of them was inevitable. But that fight never took place.

Knowing nothing of Dick Hartson's camp, Brutus was leading his starving followers toward a meadow that they hadn't visited in three weeks when he caught the smell of wood smoke. Brutus stopped, knowing the smell for what it was but not especially alarmed. The trees hid him and his nose told him that no man was dangerously near. Brutus stole to the edge of the forest.

Dick, Sable, and Croppy, with their three new burro captives, had returned less than fifteen minutes before. The five baby burros, Molasses, and Croppy, were staked along the creek. The camp was farther up, among the trees. Brutus licked his chops, but when the impetuous Rowdy would have edged past, he drove him back, and settled down to wait.

Brutus was very hungry. But with food, ample quantities of it, in prospect, he was also patient, for his leader's eye had grasped the situation. To go down into the park now, when they could be seen, would be sheerest folly. Brutus waited for the friendly cover of night, for he knew perfectly well that they could not be seen then. When the eager Rowdy tried again to launch a daylight attack, Brutus drove him back a second time. Hunger-haunted eyes fixed on the baby burros, Rowdy lay down beside Bull and did not break again.

Night came and still Brutus waited. He wanted no errors, for he knew that the wild dogs would have only one chance. They must take every advantage that offered itself. Brutus stared at Dick's fire, and only when that fire began to die did he finally rise.

He knew what they must do. The baby burros, Molasses, and Croppy, were tied. They couldn't run away, and there was no need to rush them as the pack would have rushed a faltering deer. The foals would be easy to kill, but he was not sure about Croppy. Once before the pack had attacked a horse and been the better of four hours killing it. They had better kill the young ones first and then get Molasses. If need be, they'd take on the man. The wild pack had killed one man in broad daylight; it would not be hard to kill another by night. Brutus didn't even think about Sable.

As Brutus began to run, Croppy screamed, but the dog did not hesitate. He remained the general, the leader, and knew when Dick Hartson and Sable left the fire to run toward the threatened burros. Brutus had taken the man into account and expected him to interfere.

The .22 began its snap-snap-snap and every time it did a tiny flower of flame bloomed at its muzzle, then winked out in the darkness. Brutus faltered, but his nerve would have held had not Rowdy yelped shrilly, then become suddenly silent.

Bull whirled with Brutus and the .22 continued to snap as they raced back into the forest. Brutus did not know that Dick was aiming blindly, shooting at shadows, or that the shot that killed Rowdy was a lucky one. Brutus knew only that he had responded to a momentary fear, and as soon as he was safe among the trees he realized his error. He could have reached and killed the man, and that should have been his primary objective. With him out of the way, there would have been nothing to fear. Brutus started down toward the camp for a second attack.

He was interrupted.

Hungry, betrayed by his trusted leader, and born to fight, Bull was realizing his own frustrations by turning on Brutus. The most stupid member of the wild pack, Bull's method of fighting was not clever, but peculiarly his own. He attacked with his eyes closed, got a grip with his jaws, and held on until he could get a more lethal grip, or until whatever he was fighting lay dead. But Bull hadn't fought anything except desperate, winded beasts already harried to near-exhaustion by the wild pack, and Brutus knew it.

As Bull bored in, Brutus merely slithered aside and slashed. Whimpering, but not crying out, the clumsy

Bull turned and came back. When he fought, it was always to the death. Now it was to his own death.

Brutus leaped on his back, seized Bull's neck, and ground his powerful jaws. Bull strained so hard that his front feet left the ground and pawed the air, but Brutus had his hold. There was an audible snap as Bull's neck broke, then he went limp. Brutus released his grip, and glanced back into the meadow. Although he felt no compunction about killing Bull, he whimpered his vexation. Previously, the odds had been in favor of another immediate attack. Now everything was against it.

While he had been fighting with Bull, Dick Hartson had built another fire. It glowed near the creek, and a shower of sparks floated into the air as Dick threw a great armload of branches on it. By its light Brutus could see Dick and Sable clearly. The flames' friendly glow also enveloped Molasses and the five foals. Brutus licked his chops and studied the scene.

If he went back now, he faced certain failure and knew it. When he attacked again, and he had every intention of doing so, the odds must be stacked for him. Brutus lay down to await his chance.

Dawn came, and Dick Hartson led his charges across the plateau in a compact little group. Keeping far enough away so that he could not be seen, but near enough to maintain contact, Brutus followed. That night another great fire lighted the camp and Brutus could do nothing.

He bided his time, still sure that he'd find his chance. An hour before noon, he thought he had found it.

Below the forest line, a thin little trail wandered down the side of a boulder-studded canyon. Brutus knew all about the trail, for he himself had traveled it many times. As soon as he saw Dick start down it,

Brutus stopped following and faded into the rocks and ledges.

He began to run, treading various paths he knew, and the next time he appeared on the canyon's side he was both far down the trail and directly above an eight-foot ledge upon which grew some sprigs of sage. Brutus slunk out on the ledge and crouched down, motionless.

He had planned well. The trail ran so close to the ledge that various animals, traveling the canyon, often left hair caught on the ledge. It would be easy to leap on whatever passed. Brutus looked up the trail and saw the procession coming, Sable and Dick in the lead, Molasses next, and the five foals crowding in the rear.

TAWNY was both heartsick and fighting mad. Turning back to help Sable, he had seen Brutus throw him. Knowing nothing of Dick's rescue of the collie, Tawny believed that the wild pack had killed his friend, and he was filled with a burning desire to even that score.

In addition, he had a grudge of his own. Twice he had met the wild pack and both times they had attacked him. Tawny was through being hunted or driven. The issue must be settled.

Sleeping when he was weary, catching a jack rabbit when he was hungry, he had roamed purposefully over the plateau. His head was always up and his eyes were forever roving. In his relentless search for the wild pack, he saw and investigated everything that moved.

When he found no trace of the quarry he sought, he widened his area of search. Thus it was that, just before noon, he stood far up on the opposite side of the canyon down which Dick Hartson was traveling. He saw Dick and the burros come around a curve where the trail bent close to the canyon's wall. He did not see Sable because the collie had lingered behind to sniff at a dead jack rabbit. Before he appeared. Tawny had turned his eyes toward something else.

On the slope above the ledge, he had seen motion. Even if they had noticed, few other dogs would have given it a second glance. Only a keen-eyed greyhound would have clearly seen Brutus coming down the slope, crawling out on the ledge, and crouching down there.

Tawny's eyes glowed fiercely, but he wasted no breath in growling or snarling as he began the most important race of his life. He kept his head up, his eyes fixed on the ledge where Brutus lay, as he started the grueling run that led clear to the floor of the canyon and halfway up the opposite side.

11. Last Meeting

When the wild pack made its night attack on his camp, Dick Hartson hadn't known at first just what the danger was. All he had seen were shadows against the dark outline of the forest in the background, and there seemed to be dozens of them. Then he began shooting, and when the stricken Rowdy yelped Dick knew his attackers.

He steadied. The camp was being rushed by dogs, not werewolves or ghouls. But in another way that very fact was almost as unnerving. Dick, who prided himself on knowing dogs, would have sworn that, after the encounter in the park, no member of the wild pack would ever again venture near a human being. But here they were, although he had no idea as to how many there might be. He could not be sure whether or not the wild dogs he'd seen before were merely a roving band from a much larger pack that was now attacking in full force, or even that these were the same dogs. He was inclined to believe they were not, for the dogs in the meadow had taken fast flight after they knew a human was near.

Suddenly Dick was struck by the chilling thought that Tawny not only might be, but probably was, with the attacking pack. Although he did not want to believe it, the possibility put the whole situation in a much clearer light. Beyond doubt these dogs were led and inspired by some devilishly intelligent and cunning creature, and the greyhound was certainly intelligent enough. Dick shuddered. Having no way of knowing that he was dealing with hungry animals that really wanted the burros, he thought himself their objective.

After building up a second fire, he felt better. But not until dawn brightened and individual trees became distinct in the forest did Dick let his fires go out. Then he saw the dead Rowdy lying in the park, and knew he was dealing with the same dogs he had seen before.

Croppy was gone and his loss was felt. But rather than mourn that which could not be helped, it was better to take positive action about that which could. First of all, he'd have to take the burros to safety.

Dick set his jaw grimly. If it were not for careless or thoughtless people, the wild pack would never have existed. But it did, and had become a deadly menace. Dick knew that he must report the pack as soon as he could, and try to bring a game warden or ranger back with him. Failing, he himself would have to hunt the wild dogs. And if Tawny was one of them, he could not be excepted. Sooner or later, if the wild pack continued to range freely, there would be tragedy on this plateau.

So intent on the forest that he never looked away for more than a few seconds at a time, the nervous Sable would venture no more than his own length from Dick. That meant that the wild dogs were still awaiting their chance. Dick stooped to pet Sable's ears and considered what he should do. Croppy was gone. Although he had undoubtedly made his way back to the ranch and would be safe there, his absence was awkward. Dick would have to walk and lead the burros. Well, they had better start.

Dick broke camp and packed his equipment on Molasses. Leading the burro, he started out across the plateau, the five young foals tagging along willingly.

Sable whined, and stayed close at hand. Dick didn't like that. He had hoped that, when they left the camp, they'd also leave the wild dogs behind. Seeing their quarry escaping, they might go about their affairs. Instead, as Sable's nervousness revealed plainly, they were following. It was almost as unnerving as the previous night's attack.

Dick halted Molasses, pulled his axe from beneath the pack ropes, and tightened the ropes again. When they went on, he kept the axe in his hand. The rifle held only six cartridges, and should he use all of them he wanted a weapon more formidable than a clubbed .22 rifle.

He chose their line of travel with great care and tried at all times to remain in the most open forest. When young evergreens or thickets blocked their path, he went around them, even though doing so meant going yards out of their way. Such places were ideal ambushes, and if the wild dogs attacked he wanted to be in a position to shoot as many as possible before resorting to the axe.

Dick stopped an hour before his usual camping time, partly because they were near a water hole but largely to collect a great quantity of wood. He wanted no repetition of last night, when he'd had to stumble around in darkness to gather fuel. Even if Sable's actions had not told him that danger was still near, Molasses' unwillingness to venture out of the firelight was evidence enough. Very wise, Molasses knew where he was best off. Dick staked the five foals where they could reach such grass as was available and still have the fire's protection, and made ready for the night.

He was more tired than he remembered ever having

been before, and at the same time he dared not sleep.
He got up to walk around the fire while Sable tagged
close beside him. The impulse to sleep overcome, Dick
sat down on a chunk of firewood. Head on his paws,
Sable snoozed.

. After an age, morning came, and when it did Dick felt
better. He'd made it through last night, yesterday, and
the night before, and when the sun again went down
he'd be safe at the C-2.

It was with a feeling of vast relief that he finally
emerged from the forest into open country. There were
hiding places here: tumbled boulders, crevices,
clumps of sage or greasewood. But there weren't nearly
as many, and if the wild dogs still intended to attack,
they would not be able to get close before he saw them.

Molasses halted to pluck a succulent bit of grass
growing beside the trail, and when Dick tried to pull
him on, the burro braced his feet and wouldn't move.
Dick's hopes took an upward swing. Until now he had
not only had no trouble whatever in keeping Molasses
near, but he couldn't have driven him away. If the wild
dogs had finally abandoned the hunt, Molasses and
Sable would be the first to know. Dropping his hand to
pet Sable's head, and not finding him, Dick looked
around. The collie had gone ten or fifteen feet from the
trail. Legs stiff, tail wagging, and head bent, he was
snuffling with absorbed interest at a gopher's den. Dick
forgot his weariness.

He'd won! The very fact that Sable and Molasses
would again act natural was proof of that. Dick grinned
as he thrust the axe back beneath Molasses' pack ropes.

"You can carry it now," he said happily. "I won't
need it any more."

The rifle dangling from his hand, he continued down
the trail. Suiting his pace to Molasses', he looked ahead
and noticed the ledge. With that on one side and a

boulder-littered slope on the other, the trail was very narrow. But a good horse would have no trouble, and burros could certainly make it.

Sable had lingered somewhere back up the trail and Dick was directly beneath the ledge when Molasses pulled back on the lead rope. Muttering, Dick turned to discipline the recalcitrant burro.

He did not see Brutus leap. He was aware of nothing until, suddenly, the wild dog's full weight sent him sprawling. Vaguely he heard Molasses snort and pound away, and the lesser sounds of the babies. The rifle flew from his hand, and there was a metallic bounce as it fell on the rocks. Struggling to his feet, he saw Brutus. The Alsatian's leap had carried him part way down the slope but he was clambering back up, snarling.

Then Dick was aware of another dog rushing up over the wall of the canyon and hurling itself on Brutus. It was the greyhound.

Down the slope, a dozen feet from the trail, the two dogs were moving so swiftly and changing positions so fast that where one stood now, the other stood in a split second. Equally matched, neither had the advantage.

Dick snatched up his rifle but did not dare shoot. He must get Brutus, but they were fighting so furiously and moving so fast that he might shoot Tawny. Tense, but ready for his opportunity the second it offered, Dick waited.

Suddenly, and with no advance warning, Brutus flung himself away from Tawny, whirled, and tensed himself to spring. Dick squeezed the trigger. Brutus took two forward steps, then slumped down, dead from a lucky heart shot.

The panting, gasping Tawny looked once at his enemy, then glanced back at Dick. Dick stood motionless, understanding the struggle going on in this dog who had learned the wild ways of lonely survival. Then he spoke softly.

"You can run if you like and I'll not lift a hand to hurt or stop you. But both of us want the same things and I think we'd be great partners. How about it?"

Tawny stood his ground as Dick started slowly toward him. Then, wriggling with joy, Sable bounded up to lick Tawny's face.

ABOUT THE AUTHOR

JIM KJELGAARD's first book was *Forest Patrol* (1941), based on the wilderness experiences of himself and his brother, a forest ranger. Since then he has written many others—all of them concerned with the out-of-doors. *Big Red, Irish Red,* and *Outlaw Red* are dog stories about Irish setters. *Kalak of the Ice* (a polar bear) and *Chip, the Dam Builder* (a beaver) are wild-animal stories. *Snow Dog* and *Wild Trek* describe the adventures of a trapper and his half-wild dog. *Haunt Fox* is the story both of a fox and of the dog and boy who trailed him, and *Stormy* is concerned with a wildfowl retriever and his young owner. *Fire-Hunter* is a story about prehistoric man; *Boomerang Hunter* about the equally primitive Australian aborigine. *Rebel Siege* and *Buckskin Brigade* are tales of American frontiersmen, and *Wolf Brother* presents the Indian side of "the winning of the West." The cougar-hunting *Lion Hound* and the greyhound story, *Desert Dog,* are laid in the present-day Southwest. *A Nose for Trouble* and *Trailing Trouble* are adventure mysteries centered around a game warden and his man-hunting bloodhound. The same game warden also appears in *Wildlife Cameraman* and *Hidden Trail,* stories about a young nature photographer and his dog.